CAMOUFLAGE

T.J. GERLACH

LITHIC PRESS
FRUITA, COLORADO

CAMOUFLAGE
T.J. GERLACH
ISBN 978-1946-583-055
Lithic Press

LITHIC PRESS
fine books for an old planet

www.lithicpress.com

AUTHOR'S NOTE

The majority of the pieces in this book are the result of an exercise I invented which is a loose version of the process typically called a die-cut. I read through a book and make a list of words used in that book. With this vocabulary, I write a piece based on those words. It feels like my voice blends with the voice of the original, and also that the original blends with mine. Hence the term "camouflage."

CONTENTS

CAMOUFLAGE

SHALE

(Camouflage Don DeLillo, *Mao II*, "At Yankee Stadium")

They're traveling to a state with shale. A state in which she is staying no longer than it takes to drop him off with the other men. Men who are nomads. Dead-eyed. American but fixed to eight words of English. He tries not to think about it. Instead he focuses on the bright colors of her clothes as she tickles eighty on the interstate. The clothes match her candy-yellow Camry.

When night descends the motel they find is cheap-looking, cheap-smelling, but not inexpensive. Next motel might be fifty miles up the road and better, or a couple hundred and worse. The ice machine is busted. Which is OK. He doesn't need ice for his drinks and this way its hum is guaranteed not to seep through the walls. Funny how the smallest things can amplify at night.

He takes those doily things off two glasses and fills them both with generous pours of tequila. She does a line on the nightstand. Her method is memorized, mechanical. She motions like does he want some? He shakes his head. His guess is there will be plenty of everything with the diggers and the riggers.

When he comes out of the shower the TV is on. He turns it off along with the lights. The moon, silver and crimson, drips into the room. "I wish there was music," she says as she lays back on the bed. He agrees. Music, the vast arc, the continuous wave. How it covers over open spaces.

Sex is like a toy--funny and rudimentary. Sweaty play. For a while he forgets who he is. Then the deep spasm arrives. His head hasn't even hit the pillow before he feels himself zooming out and away. First to the ceiling, then the sky, and then space, galaxies, the universe. She reaches for the remote and turns on the TV. Distance is contagious.

DUSK

(Camouflage William Faulkner, *Absalom, Absalom!* in dialog
with Ernest Hemingway, *A Moveable Feast*)

Almost sundown. Another dead-end to another dead afternoon. The whole town beneath the notice of most everything
but the sun. Sunset is sunlight hyper distilled. At its best when
crowded with cloudy ghosts.

A place of motorcycles and trucks. Hard-pressed to find a
car that wasn't just passing through. The town locked in by live-
stock, horses, cattle and mules. The far off mountains remain
outside the known world, sitting at the horizon like a monas-
tery.

He wooed her by his masculine solitude. His tobacco chew-
ing. His smiling teeth. Leaning against a wall, one foot on it,
the other on the ground. At his desk he drew in a notebook
with an intensity where you knew for him the four walls of the
classroom were gone. Teachers didn't even bother to call him
out on it. When she finally saw the insides of the notebook
it was just conjectural covers for imaginary bands, along with
silhouetted naked women. Like mud flaps or the signs for strip
bars.

He insisted on marriage, even before he'd laid her, or even laid eyes on her naked opulence. She was a girl. Newly minted.

No church. No ceremony. No cake of infantile enormity. No band cursed with instruments that had to play every request. Just their truck turned into a carriage, tied with cans and tennis shoes. Windows soaped.

She'd had fun here. Or a past here. The past was like a summons—it pulled you in regardless of circumstances. Her favorite was exploring the abandoned auto repair shops with their beautifully detailed junk. Inside barns, the high beams and wide insides, they were dolls in dollhouses. Mirrored like Alice. What she wouldn't give to have a snapshot of her and her friends back then. Their skillful "borrowing" of racy books from the town's bookstore. Covers with long-haired, big-chested men. Pages that taught them to be welcoming.

Now she was an anonymous wife. Soon, no doubt, to be more so with anonymous children. She hoped she'd cast herself in the right story. Worrying if what she'd thought were crystals were really just his eyes. The only difference between bachelor and husband was now she shared his solitude. He spent his days in town, involving himself with the basements of old, tall buildings.

Yet still coming back looking sunburned.

Some nights, some mornings, not many, he was there. Five minutes and then asleep with his legs hanging off the bed, feet aimed at the floor, like he might have to run.

She stayed sitting, looking out the window long after the sun was gone. Drunkards pissing in the alley. A woman using the street as a squat toilet. Life is not written. It is suffered. She could get up and go. It's a good thing to think of going.

FIGHT

(Camouflage Don DeLillo, *Mao II*, Chapter 6)

It's been part of their lives since they were introduced to the concept of recess. Twenty minutes of freedom from brain-washing. Probably why they still meet near playgrounds. Ten yards away there are jungle gyms and see-saws painted in bright acrylics with a puckered ground you can't hurt yourself on. Play. How you need it to separate the monotony. Sometimes when they are bored they use cigarettes to give themselves these anonymous, gumdrop tattoos. There are half-a-dozen puffy, red welts on his arms.

When they fight punches are directed to the upper-body and face. No kicking; no wrestling on the patchy grass. This is not a code. No more than your knee's compulsory kick is a code when thumped with a doctor's mallet. They're upright architecture, two solid columns against the leaky landscape, the unreadable cloud-banded sky. Below-the-belt is fair game. Something gargoylish about genitals. A dozen hanging in the steam and churchy tile acoustics of the shower after gym.

He feels his leanness, his paleness, his solitude. His skin

buttery with sweat. He's always alone after the first few punches. So laughably nameless it's like he's fighting himself. He gets hit in the midsection and his body deflates for a moment. Knuckles catch the side of his head. He bites his tongue and the jelly of blood fills his mouth. It clots like vomit on his lips. Some people are sitting far away on the playground equipment, drinking beer and smoking pot. Most have gathered around the two fighters. They make, with arbitrary equations, an impromptu ring. They stand, or sit cross-legged, or lean back on tightening haunches. He will hurt and be hurt. The suspense comes from finding out who will be first to lose consciousness, to feel that deep-reaching stillness.

EVERYONE IS FROM THE PAST

(Camouflage Frederick Barthelme, *Moon Deluxe,* in dialog
with Roland Barthes, *The Neutral*)

He says, "Everyone is from the past."

On a large piece of cardboard she has traced letters in glue and sprinkled them with glitter. It is taped to a wall, but the wall is too far across the room to read it without his glasses.

"It was disturbing to see him. Like time travel," she says.

"Time travel is always a bust," he says. "Everything grows in memory. More overwhelmingly perfect."

There are speakers the size of steamer trunks in the other room but he's never heard her say anything about music. When they are in the car, she pushes the button to turn off whatever he has going.

She gets up and starts for the kitchen. He takes a sip of the cold dregs at the bottom of his coffee mug just to have something to do with his mouth.

"You busy? Want to take a ride?" he says loud enough for it to travel through the kitchen wall.

"What's there to see?" she calls back. He hears water running. Utensils doing something.

"We can go to the mountains or the city."

She teaches high school history. She's twenty-seven, tall, with eyes the color of oysters, strong cheekbones, and too-large front teeth. What he'd like is a nice long drive. What he'd like is to get her into a motel swimming pool.

"I'm weary," she says.

He wonders at her use of a word like that. *Weary.* It's like an awkward contraption from the Victorian Age. But it is also so her.

"I'll drive," he says, "I'll drive slow. You can just sit there. Sleep if you want. We'll drive calmly into the dark, ramble toward midnight. Doesn't that sound nice?"

The phone rings. She goes to the bedroom to get it.

"This talk we've had? Has it helped?"

There's no reply. Just the murmur of another conversation.

TYPING

(Camouflage Don DeLillo, *Mao II*, Chapter 10)

The astonishment of hammers drumming. Each letter is
the shadow of an electric shiver zippering the everyday to paper. Bruised paper sun-stained and taut. Sentences a charcoal
horizon in the firm-footed weather of ink.

EASTER EGGS

(Camouflage Tom Robbins, *Still Life with Woodpecker*)

Tonight the bunny itch got to me late. My daughter had long since gone to bed when I made my way to the kitchen. I got a half dozen coffee mugs and filled them with food coloring and vinegar to bejewel a handful of hard boiled moons. They were peacock purple, blue, red and green. A bubblegum pink. One yellowing to the color of sunbeams. As they soaked I popped the cork on a bottle to have myself a drink. When they are done, dried, I'll stroll slowly through the yard like I'm an actor in a silent movie. Half think I might go blindfolded because as I chipmunk around the yard I'll look for places to hide the fat, little colored toads of love from myself.

DEEP BLUE

My weed guy was leaving town but he'd arranged for me to meet some other dude who had weed and some Oxy and some other stuff besides. I was driving through unfamiliar streets, a part of town I hadn't been to much. No particular reason just that even in a town this small you develop your patterns, your haunts, your habits. I was headed to this new guy's house, checking the address I was given against the streets and numbers I was going past when I saw it. A Harley Davidson Super Glide with a fuel tank bluer than night. It had a piece of cardboard resting on the seat with a phone number and a price and it only took once around the block for me to memorize them both. That night I called the number. Hold it for a month, I said to the man who answered, and I'll give you $250 more than you're asking. Talk to you in four weeks, he said.

I was never much of one for work. I'd pick up stuff here and there when I needed to and once I got a bit flush I'd quit. More often than not I'd manage to leave the job with an "injury" of one sort or another so government assist helped ease the glide back into unemployment. But the next morning, after seeing that bike, I drove straight over to the Alpha Beta where they'd had a Help Wanted sign taped to the sliding glass doors since

Halloween. I told them I'd take as many hours as they cared to give me.

The Alpha Beta had been around forever. They had been one of the first grocery stores in town but also one of the smallest. Then the city built the new high school just three blocks away and they started doing some serious business. They put in a new counter up front and stocked it up like a gas station. Chips, candy, hot dogs, the kind of stuff that kids could load up on over lunch and after school. That's where they stuck me most of the time. It was considered a low man on the totem pole kind of thing since you had to put up with all those kids. But I didn't mind. I just got high and helped myself to all the free Slush Puppies I could want.

But when there was something else to be done, like mopping up some mess, or emptying a pallet that had just come in, Doug Standard, the manager would relieve me of my counter duties and I'd be sent off to see to it. One of those things was herding carts. For the size of the store, Alpha Beta's parking lot was pretty damn big and there were always a million carts scattered all over it. They had a rack toward the front of the store where people were supposed to put them. It had a little sign that said "Thank You For Your Courtesy." But no one ever used the rack. At best they might aim a cart at it from about twenty yards away and give it a push. Those never came close to anything except some old Buick or Chrysler that had been dumb enough to park nearby.

I liked herding. Maybe it looked foolish for a grown man in his thirties to be out there doing a kid's job, but I could take my time, have a cigarette, roll up my shirt sleeves and feel the sun on my arms. I liked to see how big a train I could get going. My best was fourteen which if you do the math added up to fifty-six of those wobbly wheels wanting badly to go with the downward slope of the parking lot. It was about all you could do just to hang on.

I'd been working a couple of weeks when I started noticing one particular car out in the parking lot. It was a little red

Camry and always seemed to be parked in the same place—last row, far right side. There was a girl in it. Sometimes there was a friend or two with her, but usually she was alone. I tried not to think too much on it but I could swear she was watching me. So when fate left a cart not three cars away from hers I decided to approach. She looked a little nervous but rolled down her window.

"Watcha doin'?" I asked.

She shrugged.

"Homework."

I looked over and sure enough there was a pile of books on the passenger side.

"Yeah? Why here?"

"Helps me think."

"How 'bout the library? Or home?"

She shook her head.

"I like it here. Is that OK?"

"Sure," I said. "I guess. Whatever you want."

I added the stray cart to the others I'd gathered and went back inside the store.

I'd kind of recognized the girl. She had definitely been in the store some. Real pretty but shy. School let out at 2:10 and by 2:20 you could have a dozen or more girls in the store. You might not think it but the girls were rowdier than the boys. The boys played it cool, their attention split between the girls and casing out something they might could steal. But the girls would throw up a racket, always laughing and hugging and kissing like they been separated by many years and maybe even an ocean or two. This involved them drawing a lot of attention to their bodies and they made sure you got an eyeful. The performance was for their own benefit, but they needed someone else to see it for it to really count. So a shy type like the Camry girl wasn't going to stand out much. But now that I'd seen her up close, talked to her, I found that I was thinking on her real hard.

The next day, Doug Standard sent me out for carts at 1:30.

Too early for her to be there and late enough that I worried the next time he'd send me out she'd have come and gone. So I left a half dozen carts out there and sure enough at 2:45 Doug sent me out again. There she was, back right corner. I didn't even bother with the pretense of carts, I just went over.

"I forgot to ask your name yesterday," I said.

"Katherine."

"Mike," I said and reached through the window. We shook hands and I felt her touch go right up my arm and into my chest.

"What's your homework today?"

"English," she said. "Shakespeare."

"Wow, you must be smart."

"Everybody has to read it."

"But a lot of them probably just read about it on the internet or rent the movie or something. I'll bet you really read it."

She smiled.

"Yeah, I do."

So on each day after that my cart herding breaks at Alpha Beta got longer and longer as I'd go and meet with Kat. I wasn't worried too much about getting fired. The money for Deep Blue, which was the name I'd given the motorcycle the first day I saw it, was accumulating plenty fast. If anything maybe too fast because now that I'd found Kat I had some mixed feelings about the job coming to its inevitable end.

We'd sit in her car and talk. I kept to just cigarettes which I tried to coax her into but she didn't like them. As a show of good faith though she'd sometimes go ahead and hold one, her hand near the window, just letting the ember creep down the length of the cigarette until the cigarette was nothing. With her other hand she'd point out interesting things to me in her textbooks, of which there were a lot, because I had been right, she was real smart.

When the time came I called the guy with the bike to make sure he was good to his word. He was. I drove out to his place and handed him the cash in an envelope with the Alpha Beta logo in the top left corner. He thumbed the bills.

"It's all yours," he said before adding, "How you getting it home?"

I hadn't thought of that but now I saw what he meant. If I drove the bike home my car would be stranded out at his place. But if I drove my car, of course, I wouldn't have the bike. I knew there was an answer. At school or somewhere there had been a riddle like this. It was about a raft and a fox and a chicken or something—a bunch of animals that would eat each other. The question was how were they to ride on the raft together to get to the other side of the river without gobbling each other up.

"Give me the keys," I said. "I'll come get it tomorrow."

The next day I arrived three hours late for my shift and told Alpha Beta I quit. Then I stood outside the store smoking until Kat arrived. I'd figured out the raft thing.

"Where's your shirt?" she said, meaning the green polo all the Alpha Beta employees wore.

"Quit," I said.

"Oh," she said. And I knew it wasn't a word, not even a syllable really. Just a sound. The sound of disappointment.

"But there's something I need your help on."

I gave her my address. Asked if she knew where that was. She nodded her head and then we both drove to my place, her in her car, me in mine. I parked at the curb and got into her car, the two of us tossing books into the backseat to make room for me. Then I directed her to the house where Deep Blue was.

"Wow," she said when we pulled up. "That's yours?"

"Is now," I said, getting out of the car. "I'll meet you back at my place."

Deep Blue was as good as I'd hoped if not better. I opened up the engine and flew down the streets, weaving in and out of traffic. When I got back to my apartment building Kat was nowhere to be seen. That's how good Deep Blue was. So I sat on it idling, listening to the motor. After a while I thought maybe it wasn't my speed, maybe I had been stood up. But just about then Kat turned the corner onto my street.

She got out and closed the door. Then she just leaned against the car and looked at me.

"Ever ride one?" I asked, killing the motor and dismounting the bike.

She shook her head.

"Go on," I said patting the now empty seat.

"I don't know how," she said.

"You don't have to ride it. Just take a seat."

I fired up the engine again and Kat used the seat to swing herself up on it and then put her hands on the handlebars. I righted the bike and gave the kickstand a nudge with my shoe. Kat sat there rocking back and forth, using her tip-toes to keep the heavy thing afloat. She looked real cute. I imagined what the engine must have felt like to her, like nothing else she could possibly imagine.

"Nice," she said.

I killed the engine, put the kickstand down but she stayed on the bike.

"So," I said. "I'm not at the store anymore."

She nodded.

I felt awkward as hell but went ahead anyways.

"I guess if we are going to see each other anymore it's going to have to be somewhere else."

"There are lots of other places people can see each other besides a grocery store," she said.

"Yeah," I said. "I guess there are."

We were both quiet for a moment. Then she said, "So that's your apartment there?" and jutted her chin out towards the building.

I looked at her real steady.

"How old are you?"

"Be eighteen in five months."

"I'm thirty-two."

Kat shrugged.

"It happens," she said.

Seventeen. I wasn't real clear if that was even legal. Of course the way I was back then legal anything didn't interest me that much.

I suppose we made an odd pair. I was interested in what I thought of as "partying," or that's the word I used when I talked to other people. But really there wasn't a whole lot that was festive about it. Dim bar rooms where maybe you might knock a few pool balls around, or if you were lucky, maybe someone would start yelling at the TV and you'd have some entertainment for a few minutes until the bartender got him calmed down. Or else there were the houses of friends. Weed or something more, or both, and video games, and music turned up 'till the neighbors couldn't take it, and not remembering when it was you fell asleep, waking up on the floor in the early a.m.s.

I'd take just about any drug but my real thing was alcohol. Alcohol was something I took seriously. I had drinking down to an art, a science, or to use a phrase a guy in a bar once taught me, when it came to drinking I was *tres au fait*.

Kat, for her part, never touched anything. Certainly not drugs. The only drinks I ever saw her have were the mudslides over at Applebee's which I'm not sure are even actually considered drinks since they never bothered to I.D. her.

Kat didn't have an interest in any of that because Kat was driven. She was set for graduation in June and she had already been accepted, not to the crappy local college which was a kind of sad sinkhole on the north end of town, but to a university three states over. Even so, with all her smarts and plans, she was still a girl in a lot of ways. She always wanted movies. And not on DVD either but in an actual theater with popcorn and that stuff they let you pump on it. She wanted dancing too but I put my foot down there. To sort of make that up to her I'd take her to this one Italian place that was phony as a three dollar bill but which she'd get all giddy about and call it "romantic." But here's a real good example of what I'm talking about. How she was still a kid in some ways. Her and her friends saw this thing about yarn bombing on the internet and for about a month you never saw her without a pair of knitting needles near by. Yarn bombing is this thing like graffiti but instead of using spray paint you use yarn. Their big achievement was knitting over most of the branches on a tree over in the park. She was super proud when she showed me and I have to say I was pretty impressed. How they got up as high as they did I'll never know. And the tree was real pretty, a big rainbow, like spring had come early and had dropped acid or something.

So we went together. Dated, I guess in our way. At first I could only see her on weekdays, after school, and she had to be home by six. But then she worked it so Friday and Saturday nights were OK although she was supposed to have a curfew. I suppose it was as much my fault as hers that we broke it so often. I didn't sleep much when she was over, but I'd lay in bed looking at her face, stroking her arm, knowing I had to wake her up but thinking just five more minutes and then five more and so on until it was well past midnight.

I don't know if she told her parents about me. Or if so, how much. The truth was I really didn't want to know. I figured talking about it would just jinx it. School was out in June, then we'd have some of the summer until she had to go to the university. And while I wasn't looking forward to that day, I figured that what I had was way more than a guy like me deserved.

Then my mom died.

She'd been diagnosed with cancer a couple years back. They traced it to the silicone in some faulty implants. Or at least traced it enough so that the company that made the implants gave her a chunk of money. I don't know. We didn't talk much. She followed some guy down to Florida. After that she may as well have been on the moon.

I didn't even know she was dead until I got a letter telling me to go talk to this lawyer in town. He told me the news and about how the money from the settlement, or what was left of it, was mine now. He said a number that was pretty damn big.

"How are you feeling?" Kat asked when I told her about it all. I guess she probably meant about my mom not the money.

"I'm feeling like buying something," I said.

What I bought was a house. Well, a trailer. But I owned it and not only that I owned the land that it sat on—half an acre out close by the river. Real pretty out there. You could practically fish by casting a reel out one of the back windows. Although what the hook would come back with might be a tad suspect.

People say that owning a house changes a person and I'd have to agree. I did feel different, and what I felt was horny. Kat may have had her college and all that but now I had something too. Let's face it. My old place wasn't exactly a chick magnet. There was this ring that never came off the inside of the toilet, an oven that didn't work and had no door anyway, there were holes in the front door that people always thought were bullet holes but I was pretty sure upon close examination were not. But this new place had clean carpets, a dishwasher, a big shower and a tub that was deep enough that the water would come up close to your knees and not just cover your ankles like the old one. I mean the place even *smelled* good. Women would flock to it. I figured there'd be a different one every night and all the booze would be top shelf.

So things were looking good—and of course things can only be good for so long until they go bad.

Jail wasn't any big deal in our town. It wasn't "prison" or anything like that and it was nothing like the correctional facility over in Tompkins. Jail was just a place they kind of put you when they didn't know what else to do with you. Like the penalty box in hockey. In fact I've seen guys do worse stuff on the ice than some of the things I've gone to jail for.

This time was just plain bad luck. It was Kat's birthday and her parents had driven her and some of her friends over to the lake. They'd rented a cabin and they were going to spend the weekend cooking hotdogs and jumping off of piers or whatever it is people do at lakes.

I was not invited and needless to say this made me feel about as worthless as could be so I started my own little "party" at about ten o'clock in the morning. I sat there in my new place drinking, watching TV, Deep Blue calling me the whole time from the driveway.

There's nothing quite as good as drinking and driving. In fact for a long time I honestly couldn't believe it could be illegal the two of them went together so well. But the only thing better than drinking and driving is drinking and driving at night. So I waited, and when the sun went down, just a watermelon strip left on the horizon, I filled a flask and got my keys.

Everybody knows the pleasures of a bike, even if you've never been on one. You got the engine, the wind, the headlight dancing on the interstate up in front of you. I got a pretty good ways out of town when all of a sudden I had to pee something fierce. So I started looking for a good place on the side of the road to pull over. Then, just right up ahead, I saw the Telford exit and the benevolent glow of Burger King.

I want to point out that I was trying to do the right thing, but by the time I pulled in to Burger King the situation had grown a little desperate. I don't even remember turning off Deep Blue. I just hustled myself inside as quickly as humanly possible where I opened the door on to the most god awful disgusting bathroom I had ever seen. I mean the stuff I recognized was bad enough, but there were things in there that to this day I wonder exactly what they could have been.

You know, it didn't even occur to me to go ahead and try the women's? Here I was drunk off my ass on a motorcycle. Something not only illegal but probably some sort of sin as well. And yet the taboo of the ladies room still held sway over me. So instead I went out around back, over by the dumpsters, unzipped and proceeded. The lights hit me from behind almost immediately. I knew what it was right away so I didn't turn around. The center of my universe right then was the tranquility coming over me as the urine vacated my bladder. I went ahead and finished my business, gave a big sigh, zipped up and walked over to the squad car.

Most of what followed was a formality. When you are caught peeing in the parking lot of a Burger King it's surely as good an indication of public intoxication as a breathalyzer or backward recitation of the alphabet. So it was that, public intoxication and lewdness. I objected to the lewdness.

"Listen," the officer said. "Technically I could write it up as a sex crime."

"What does taking a piss have to do with sex?" I said.

"Well, sir, your dick, or rather, penis was outside of your pants."

So those two with my priors—a couple other public intoxications, a possession, a petty theft and half a dozen unpaid speeding tickets—all added up to thirty days which I could get down to twenty with good behavior.

When Kat got back from the lake she came and visited everyday. She kept telling me it was OK, that I just hit a rough patch. "It's to be expected," she said. "You're mourning." It took me a second to process what she meant by that. "You've suffered a loss," she said, meaning my mom I now understood. "And yes, your freedom has been taken away too, but just temporarily."

I'd never had a woman visit me in jail before, so I didn't know how they were supposed to act. But Kat was so damn upbeat that I could have sworn she was almost glad I was in there. Jail's been known to bring clarity and while maybe I wasn't a hundred percent clear it felt like something was up that I wasn't in on.

Sure enough the second week she came in looking good. I mean she always looked good but this was better even than normal. She was dressed-up super nice and wearing her make-up in that sexy way that made you think she wasn't wearing any at all. Visitations were held at fold-up tables and chairs in the rec room and when she came in you could feel the other guys, and even the women they were with, all sort of shift in their seats.

This was it, I thought. She's leaving me. You don't go around looking like that unless it's for someone else. In the two weeks I'd been in the cooler she'd gone and found herself another man.

She sat down and smiled real big. I folded my arms across my chest pushed back in the chair so that I rocked on the two back legs.

"Our luck has changed," she said.

"How's that?" I asked, thinking that someone wasn't going to be feeling too lucky when I bashed his face in the moment I got released.

"I'm pregnant."

Her saying that just about knocked me off my feet, literally, I had to grab forward and catch the table to keep from falling ass backward in the chair. Pregnant. One month and two days along. We hugged and kissed as far as the jail's regulations would allow us. Holding her and feeling her body like that against mine I started having semi-conjugal thoughts. But then I said hold on. You can't have thoughts like that about a pregnant woman and that's what Kat was all of a sudden. We sat back down across from each other. Kat was smiling and crying and laughing all at once. "Aren't you happy," she said and I nodded. But the truth was my mind was having a hard time wrapping itself around the whole deal.

The one thing jail gives you plenty of is time. Our "cells" weren't what most people thought. It wasn't a wall of bars and people clanging metal cups against them all day. They were more like offices. Just regular square boxes with a thick door with a window in the middle made out of some sort of heavy plastic or plexiglass or some such material. Anyway, my bed faced that window and as I sat there looking at it for hours on end I noticed, or not noticed, but had it just kind of register for the first time, that the window had these thin cross-hatches of metal inside it. Thin as thread. And no matter that they didn't look the part, those were sure enough bars. Which made it not really a window. Mike, I said to myself, I don't care how often you've been in here, you are a man of windows not bars.

That's when life stopped feeling like one long detour to me. I had a double sentence now. The first, the one from the legal system was going to be over in a little over a week. But this other sentence was a lifer. It was like a clock, or no, an hourglass because instead of a battery you could take out, or a plug you could pull, this one was all sand and gravity and there was no stopping those.

"What about school?" I asked Kat at one point.

"School can wait," she said.

Well maybe, I thought. Good for her, she had choices. Well, I figured, I had the right to some choices too. I wasn't the kind of person who would up and leave a woman while she was pregnant. I'd see her through that. And I'd see that she and the baby got settled and all in a place of their own. But one thing I wasn't going to do was to give up that trailer and all those future women it held.

While my plan was smooth on the inside, in the outside world it proved more sticky. I had six days left in jail when Kat came to visiting hours crying. I got it out of her that she'd finally told her parents about me, about us, about the baby. Seems they'd taken the news pretty badly. What was I to do? I mean I felt kind of responsible.

"Don't worry about them," I said. "I can sign over my keys to you here. There's three. The biggest one is the trailer. Just stay there."

Kat looked up. The crying slowed down—no tears now, just some sniffling.

"Are you asking me to move in with you?" she said.

That's the thing with giving. No matter what you give it isn't enough. I'd given her a baby, and now I was giving her a roof over her head, and still she had to go and make it into an even bigger deal.

I got four days shaved off my sentence for good behavior. One of the workers brought me the clothes I'd come in with. I could still smell the exhaust of Deep Blue in the jeans. I dressed, signed some papers, and after twenty-six days was once again a free man, at least in the eyes of the law.

Deep Blue was in impound so Kat picked me up and together we drove to the trailer. I'd only lived in it for less than a month before I was carted off to jail, but even so it was totally unrecognizable. Before it hadn't been much more than a mattress, a sofa and a 55" flat screen. But Kat had gone and hunted around and found a bunch of used furniture so the place was real cozy. Everywhere I looked there was something new. For example there were pictures on the walls. And I mean real framed pictures. Not posters and tape. There was a whole nursery set-up in the spare room. Kat had put all that yarn from way back to good use with enough blankets and booties for a dozen babies. In fact, that's how I felt as I stood there taking it all in. Like I'd been yarn bombed.

But Kat wasn't done making things right for the baby. Now that she had fixed up the trailer she turned her attention to me.

The first thing was no smoking—and not just inside either. I got the secondhand thing but what, I asked her, did it matter what I did in my driveway or in town or on one of my drives, especially since it had taken me $500 just to get Deep Blue away from the police.

"It's just on you," she said. "Everywhere. And then it gets on everything. And that includes me. And I don't want that seeping into the baby by osmosis or something. You'll have to quit when it gets here so why not just do it now? A baby needs a healthy daddy."

Whatever, I thought, and just because I didn't want it to become some thing I went ahead and quit. Mostly. And mostly it wasn't that bad. But then she started in on my drinking.

"What does my drinking have anything to do with anything?" I said.

"I'm not saying stop," she said. "I'm just saying set some boundaries. Some goals. Not so much and not every night. And definitely not before noon."

It got to where it was practically all we talked about. That is when we were talking at all.

Before she got pregnant when Kat watched TV, which she didn't do that much, she'd watch the History Channel or Wheel of Fortune or some sort of brain stuff like that. But as she ballooned up and started spending most of the day and most of the night on the sofa she'd gotten hooked on these marathons of crime shows. Seems like there was always one on some channel whatever the time might be. And something of them must have rubbed off because she got real good at busting me. She marked the levels of bottles and kept track of empties in the trash. If I went out she'd smell my breath when I got back, demand to see my credit card statement online, cry until I came up with a number of drinks she believed was the truth. I tried sneaking stuff in. I thought I found every nook, every cranny, where you could be assured that a bottle would remain hidden. But she found them all. Then again, even just a fifth can seem awful big when you've got not a whole lot more than 1,000 square feet to work with.

So the fights became worse because now we didn't just have my drinking to fight about we had my deceit about my drinking to fight about too. That was the word she used, deceit, and it may look small and sweet but it sure sounds ugly when it's said aloud. I thought seriously about going back to Alpha Beta; telling Kat parole officers love jobs and besides we could use extra money with one in the oven. Both of which were true. But what I was really thinking about was all them high school girls and how they wouldn't care a fig how much I drank as long as I shared some of it with them.

But I never did. Instead Kat's graduation came around. Kat didn't want to go. The school had a system in place for her situation and she'd been doing her school work from home, so to her it was like she'd already graduated in a way—classrooms, teachers, lunch on plastic trays—all that was long in the rearview mirror. But I knew she'd regret it later and for once not thinking of myself I urged her to attend. She looked great up on the stage getting her diploma and with the gown on you couldn't hardly tell anything. She was the one bright spot in what proved to be an unbelievably long and boring ordeal. There was one speech with the title "Here There Be Dragons" which sounded like it should be good but was just a bunch of crap like all the rest. They were all about the bright future, how the world was your oyster. Yeah, I thought, a giant one. With a pearl too big for you to lift and a bivalve shell that was going to clamp down on you any second.

I finally crumpled up my program and threw it under the seat because it just made it seem longer to keep counting down how much was still left. Instead I concentrated on trying to fool my brain into thinking it was drunk. The ceremony was super early—they had to get it in before the afternoon when everybody would be passing out from the heat. I did manage to sneak two beers with breakfast though. Kat was running around getting ready so I opened a beer, sat on the couch, and after taking a long pull at it put it on the coffee table at the other end of the couch where I hoped, if she noticed it at all, she would think it was an empty from the previous night.

Kat was going out to "brunch" with her parents after the ceremony. Once again I was unwelcome. Uninvited but at least not unknown. Kat had a million pictures of us. I wondered if her parents had ever seen one. As the morning droned on I scanned the faces in the crowd wondering which ones might belong to them.

The baby was due mid-October and at the start of that month Kat bought a calendar, stuck it to the living room wall, and marked down each day with a red X leading to the 17th which was circled with a red heart. When I looked at the calendar, and it was hard to miss seeing how it was over the TV, I thought about a prisoner scratching out vertical lines on a wall in groups of five. Not even looking forward to release, just marking time.

I started spending more time away from the living room. Anywhere else inside the house too for that matter. I stayed outside where I'd taken to stashing bottles of booze under the trailer where there was a good two feet of crawl space. I'd sit out there drinking with Deep Blue, polishing the bike with a cloth diaper which is as close to fatherhood as I planned to get. I didn't drink and drive on Deep Blue anymore. I didn't want to go back to jail because as bad as things looked right now I still held out hope that at the end of Kat's pregnancy I'd somehow find my way to freedom. But I still liked to sit on Deep Blue—the engine idling, giving the throttle a good twist now and then. The noise relaxed me. Helped me think. And between it and the alcohol I could get pretty far into my own head. Which was why I didn't know how long it had been when one night I saw that Kat was standing in the front doorway, holding her belly with both hands, and screaming that her water broke.

Talk about scared. I don't know who was in more of a panic—her or me. I didn't exactly know what broken water meant only that when it happened on TV everybody freaked out. My first thought was to get them into the car. But I was hammered. So my second thought was to call an ambulance. But just sitting there waiting, doing nothing, with the baby possibly coming out right then and there, with me maybe even having to catch it, was more than I could bare.

It's the worst thing I've ever done, driving those two to the hospital in the state I was in. I tell myself that maybe the adrenalin and the cold air coming in from the windows, all four of which were down on account of Kat was sweating bullets, might have sobered me up some. But I know the truth is I was damn lucky that we got to the hospital without killing someone or getting killed ourselves. Or there's no saying it couldn't have been both.

I pulled up to the E.R. and a wheelchair took Kat away. I thought a wheelchair sounded pretty good myself right about now and looked around for one but instead a nurse started writing down on a clipboard words that were coming out of my mouth. The words seemed to be in response to questions she was asking. Then she said for me to follow her this way to the delivery room. To which I said, "Hell no!" She stood there looking at me like she didn't know what I meant so I informed her that I would not be going into the delivery room thank you very much but could she please point in the direction to where it was that I could find some coffee.

I must have downed five styrofoam cups in the waiting room during the forty-five minutes Kat was in labor. Then a nurse came out, a different one, and told me that everything had gone amazingly well. That Kat had done a great job. Did I want to go and see her and my new son?

We walked down the hall to a room where Kat was sitting up in a bed holding the baby. When the nurse turned to go and leave us some privacy I said hold on. I took out my cellphone and handed it to her. Then I walked over to Kat and took the baby in my arms. I asked the nurse if she wouldn't mind snapping a picture of the three of us and this moment.

Because you see it was at that moment that I realized for all these years I'd had a hole inside of me, and the thing that was going to fill that hole was small and pink and weighed about as much as a cantaloupe.

The first thing I do each morning is go over to Kat's side of the bed where Samuel is nestled inside his crib like a pistachio. He's sound asleep, one of his impossibly small hands shoved all the way into his mouth. The room that Kat converted into a nursery gets used sometimes for the changing table in it but mostly it's just storage for all the stuff that comes along with a baby—which is a lot. I mean the clothes alone would surprise you and then there's packs and bags for this and that, and all kinds of creams and gels, stuff you'd never think of. Like, for example, this little mini turkey baster type thing that you need for cleaning out his nose. Kat's boss, Mr. Hamsun, gave us a baby monitor as a congratulations gift, which was a nice thing to do for sure but it didn't make a whole lot of sense to hook it up in a space as small as ours. I mean nobody is going to do anything in here that somebody else isn't going to hear. Besides, we like Samuel in the room with us. I'd like him to sleep in the bed with us but Kat says that that would cause some sort of mental development problems. So that's out. Which is fine because I probably wouldn't sleep real well worrying that I might accidentally roll over in the middle of the night and crush him and we'd never get the chance to find out how he would've done with the A.B.C.s let alone the S.A.T.s.

I reach into the crib and put my hand on top of Samuel's head to feel the sweet baby heat that says that he is alive and beautiful and that the world is a good place.

In the kitchen I part the curtain to look out onto the world and my little corner of it. Today is the day Ernest is coming over and the two of us are going to finish the sprinklers. The morning is young, the sky awash in pink pastels from the just rising sun. It's been four months since I stopped drinking but I still have yet to get used to seeing these hours. In the days of booze, sunrises and breakfasts were mostly just rumors.

Samuel is still on formula but I'm determined that our house is going to be the kind of house where the family sits down in the morning for a hearty breakfast and then again at night for a home cooked dinner. I never was much of a cook but I've found that the internet is a marvelous thing. There are entire websites dedicated to families doing just that— sitting down and eating— and over the past months I've developed something of a repertoire. This morning it's biscuits with sausage gravy. I get the coffee going, fry up the sausage, have the gravy made and a minute and forty-five seconds left on the biscuits when Samuel wakes up in the other room opening the day with his best Roger Daltrey impersonation. It takes about thirty seconds before Kathryn joins in yelling about when did I think it was that I'd get around to my son. I watch the numbers tick down on the oven timer. Forty-five. Forty. Kathryn doesn't say anything more because Samuel has settled into a low gurgle, but it's something which I recognize from experience is the precursor to an encore. Twenty-five, the timer says. Twenty. Fortunately Samuel has decided to switch to a ballad; a slow, steady wail that is buying me some time. Ten and five and finally zero and the beep. I grab a towel to protect my hand, get the biscuits out and on to the stove top to cool, and then hustle into the bedroom. Kat is rolled over on her side with my pillow over her head. I scoop up Samuel and he goes quiet in an instant.

It's Sunday, which is Kat's day off of work. Whatever she chooses to do on her day off is fine by me. I may not have had many jobs but that doesn't mean I don't respect work. When we had Samuel we started burning through my mom's money at a rate that got me scared. I mean money suddenly wasn't just money. It was diapers and talc now, it was the school supplies coming a little later down the road, and it was probably a soccer camp or something if he liked that sort of thing, or science camp if he didn't, or who's to say not both? Plus who knows what else. Braces maybe. Oh yeah, and a first car. And all of that without even factoring in college. So we needed, as they say, some income coming in. Kat and I had a long talk and we decided that she would get a job for two years, to sort of stem the levy, while I would go to the community college to get the training for a job for our long term well-being.

I bring Samuel from the bedroom to the fridge where we keep pre-loaded baby bottles on a little rack we used to use for soda and beer.

"See that?" I say to Samuel. "In the refrigerator? Samuel's bottles!"

Once again thanks to the internet I read that the best thing you can do for kids is talk to them. Even when they can't talk back to you, and really don't even have any idea what it is you're saying, words have some sort of magical thing that helps them grow up smarter and just all around better. So now I'm sort of like a sportscaster—doing both the play-by-play and color for our days.

I introduce him for the thousandth time to the microwave. I explain to him again what temperature the formula needs to be. Then, when it is ready, I give it to him and he quickly latches on to the rubber nipple.

Another thing I'd read, like I said, there's just no beating the internet, is that your sense of taste and your sense of smell are connected. That they are basically the same thing. So I like to think that maybe this morning Samuel's formula is spiked with the smells of the yeasty biscuits and greasy sausage just as maybe yesterday it tasted of waffles and strawberries.

It's almost 8:30. Ernest leaves his house around nine which means he could be here in as little as forty-five minutes. With Samuel working away at his bottle, I put him on the sofa and wrap him up in a fleece blanket. I have him at an angle where he is lying down, but can also look around, and is protected on all sides. "You're a donut," I tell him. "A Samuel-filled donut."

With Samuel squared away I go to the kitchen to get breakfast set-up. Every once and awhile I remember to send recaps and highlights over toward the sofa. I set out two plates on the kitchen table, two pairs of knives with forks alongside them atop two napkins. I stack the biscuits in a nice little pyramid on a plate and set it in the middle of the table. Next to it I put one of those giant latte cups which I'm using as a makeshift gravy boat.

Then I sit down on the sofa with Samuel and wait. I can't think of anything to report since we are just sitting there. I try to think of an original story to make-up and tell him but nothing comes. So instead I summarize Pulp Fiction which is one of my favorites.

Kat never has time for breakfast on work mornings. I do get my hopes up a little though on days off. But it's hard to compete with sleep. I get that and so try and not take it personal.

At nine-o-five I go ahead and eat since Ernest is going to be here any minute now. The wait has kind of fucked the gravy but I shovel it into my mouth anyway and when I'm down to the last couple of scoops I hear Ernest's truck on the driveway's gravel. I put the dirty dishes in the sink and take Samuel in to Kat. She's awake now, but still in bed, thumbing at her cell. I prop Samuel up next to her and go out to meet Ernest.

The first day we brought Samuel home I looked around at the place and felt it needed something. I worried at it for weeks. I knew some sorts of people, like Kat's parents, looked down on trailers. But a trailer is just as much a home as a house is. I mean think about it. They've both got bedrooms with beds, kitchens with food, toilets. But then it hit me. The one thing that houses had that a trailer didn't. A lawn.

We only had the front, the backyard was all river. Still I knew a lawn was beyond me. So I called Ernest. Ernest is a guy I'd met the last time around in jail. He's older than me, probably into his sixties, which is why when I found out he was in for stealing a car I was pretty impressed.

"Foolishness," he said shaking his head. He never said anymore about it.

The two of us became friends in the way that you do when your only entertainment consists of fifteen guys sharing a 20" TV screen and a table with three puzzles, a couple of chess boards, and a game of Clue with some of the cards and all the weapons missing. We opted for chess which neither of us played well other than just knowing how the pieces moved. But it was something to do with our eyes and hands while we talked.

Ernest fixes things. That's what he'd done for a living. He'd started working in an auto garage as a teenager and then went on to hook up with a heating and cooling outfit which he did for almost thirty years. Now he's retired, but he'll fix the occasional toaster or vacuum or whatever it is that someone brings by his garage where he's set-up a little workshop. He told me that just a week before his arrest he'd rebuilt a 1923 Underwood typewriter. I thought about typewriters. How when you see one they look way more complicated than a laptop, which seems weird but also right somehow. And here was Ernest who had dismantled, cleaned, fixed and put back together one that was almost a hundred years old.

When I was in jail and going through the stuff with Kat, digesting the fact that she was pregnant and feeling trapped he talked me through it as best he could.

"You don't know how things are going to be except that they are going to be nothing like you thought," he said. He would also float out some ideas about alcohol. "Fifteen years sober and I don't miss it a bit," he said. "There's no way to win. One drink is too many and twenty's not enough."

Of course I wasn't hearing any of that back then. I was complaining, feeling sorry for myself, and in general thinking on how when my sentence was up I'd escape. I actually saw myself in my mind, underground with a spoon, tunneling into some future I couldn't quite see which, of course, is why it looked so good.

But now I was hearing everything Ernest had had to say back then. So when I got the idea for the lawn I called him up and asked if he knew anything about something like that or if not did he know somebody who did.

"I've put in a lawn or two in my time," he said.

I threw out a number I could pay him.

"How's the drinking going?" he said.

"Well," I said.

"*Well* as in you are doing a lot of it or well as in you've cut back?"

"Well as in none."

"So the lawn's for the wife and kid?"

"We aren't married but yeah."

"You put in for the hardware and equipment. You can have my time for free."

Which is how we came to do the lawn in steady Sunday intervals while Kat watched Samuel. First was a sprinkler system. Sunday #1 was mostly Ernest and a piece of graph paper, mapping the dimensions I called out to him while walking around the yard with a tape measure. Between Sunday #1 and Sunday

#2 little flags had popped-up marking the underground utility lines. Something I would have never thought of which is why it was great to have Ernest even though no actual work got done that day because Ernest had a court date. Sunday #3 we took a couple of shovels and started to dig ten inch lines for the pipes to rest in. It proved to be pretty much a bitch so Sunday #4 we rented a trencher and finished the job.

Now it is Sunday #5 and the end is in sight although it proves to be a very long day broken only by a lunch run for sandwiches and Gatorade. I lay most of the PVC, painstakingly swirling the inside of each connection with a swab of glue. Once we have enough down Ernest goes to work on the risers and the sprinklers themselves. Sunday #6 was going to be burying the pipe but we push through and by six o'clock we are done with that too.

Ernest leans against his truck and takes off the ball cap he always wears when he works—a cap worn down to the softness of a chamois with the word DEKALB across the front. He looks out over the large rectangle of dirt.

"Guess we should try her," he says.

I walk around to the side of the house where the valves are. Ernest says next Spring we can automate the thing but for now it's just by hand. I turn one of the handles a quarter to the left and hear the sound of water going around the corner of the house.

When I turn that corner what I see is a thing of beauty. Out over the yard Zone 1 is laying down an even mist of pure H2O.

I go over and slap Ernest on the back. He smiles.

"I got to get going," he says.

"Sod next week?" I say. It's in the driveway all ready to go. Big, fat rolls that remind me of that sushi you see in gas stations all the time now.

He nods

"Wouldn't miss it."

I watch his car back down the driveway and then turn on to the road. Then I go over and have a seat on the little wooden riser that allows you to get from the ground up to the front door of the trailer. This is the hard part. I've accomplished something. My eyes tell me the accomplishment is real. The ache in my muscles tells me it's true. And my mind tells me it's time to commemorate. More than anything in the world right now I want a beer. But as soon as I have that thought I realize it isn't true. There are a million things I want more than a beer. I want this sprinkler system I now have. And I want my trailer, which I'm going to stop using that word for and just say "home" because the lawn is practically done and anyway the "trailer's" mobility is largely theoretical. I want it and I want what the sunlight is doing with the water right now. And more than all of that I want the two things inside.

I go around to the side of the home and turn off Zone 1. Then I turn on Zone 2. When I get back to the front Zone 2 is doing something that, if anything, is even more beautiful than what Zone 1 did. I go inside where Kat is watching TV. Samuel is on his back on the floor gumming a wooden toy block with a purple letter W. Some of the rest of the alphabet is scattered on other blocks around him.

"Do you hear the water?" I ask Kat.

"I hear something, I guess," she says.

"It's the sprinklers. Come look."

Kat gets off the sofa and stands in the doorway looking out over the yard.

"What do you think?" I say.

"It's nice," she says. "Like humming birds." And then she goes back to the TV.

As I walk through the mud to turn off Zone 2, I think what was that? Hummingbirds? I wonder if maybe she's on something. It seems like the kind of thing that would come out of my mouth back in the days when I was on things. Nowadays Kat's often acting like she might be on something. I asked her about it and she said it's probably just postpartum which I looked up and found is something celebrities get.

I go inside and shower and change. Fresh and clean I cross

the living room to sit in the fat recliner. I pretend like I'm watching the TV but I am really looking at Kat. Her face. Trying to see if there's anything there.

The next morning is crepes filled with two different kinds of jelly and dusted with powdered sugar. It's a workday so Kat is up and even eats half a crepe between two cups of coffee. While she showers I do the dishes and at nine o'clock we pack up. I sling my book bag over one shoulder, Samuel's diaper bag— which is easily twice as big as the books—over the other. Kat picks up Samuel and the three of us head out to the car.

"We're going to the car," I say to Samuel who is up ahead but looking at me over Kat's shoulder. "It's mommy's car because Daddy's car was worth less than the new brakes it required. Well actually mommy's car is technically mommy's mommy and daddy's car. You know? Grandma and Grandpa? Who take you out to the park and ice cream? They paid for the car. Just like your ice cream! But what's important is that the car is for mommy and daddy but also for you too! So we are getting in *our* car the three of us to go to mommy's work which is…."

"Can you give it a rest?" says Kat who is buckling Samuel into the carseat. "He isn't a houseplant."

Kat doesn't really buy the whole talk-to-your-kid-as-much-as-possible thing. The last straw was when she said it was making me talk in my sleep. I can't listen to that babble all day and all night, she said. So I try and do less around her.

I load the bags in the trunk and then go around and get in the driver's seat. Kat gets in the passenger side already with the cellphone going. I'm disappointed. Commuting time can be quality time. But I don't say anything, I just remind her to fasten her seatbelt.

"I'm on something important," she says, not looking up from the little screen.

So I back down the driveway, wondering why if something's important I don't know anything about it. I do a silent monolog in my head to Samuel about the importance of safety but we aren't more than ten blocks from the house when Kat finishes her important text, throws her phone in her purse, and with a sigh buckles herself in.

Kat works in the women's section of a department store on the west side of town. There are two malls in town—the one on the west side and the one on the east. They are almost identical—they both have Sabarros, they both have Gaps for instance—but they also have slight differences—Dillard's instead of Sears, Zales instead of Kay's—which makes one the "cool" mall and the other the "lame" one. Kat works at the lame one. So the job that she doesn't like in the first place is that much more humiliating. She takes great issue with the crappy pay and the just about zero prospect of a raise. "They give us words instead of money," she says. "You know, *titles*." Katherine works Women's Casual but her official title is Assistant Buyer. Which is up from Junior Buyer which she was when she first got hired. Her immediate superior, a woman she hates more than the low pay, is Christine Atkins whose title is Associate Sales Representative. The boss of both of them, the Mr. Hamsun who gave us the baby monitor, is Regional Company Vice President of Sales and Development.

It's early, the mall doesn't open for another forty-five minutes or so, and there can't be anymore than maybe a dozen cars scattered over what has to be almost a football field's worth of asphalt. My fingers twitch a little on the steering wheel and suddenly I'm very aware of my right foot. In the old days I would have given the speedometer a little ride, maybe even thrown in a donut or two. Kat would have yelled at me but in that good way that says behind the yell is a little excitement too. But instead I just gently slide up to the store's double glass doors.

"Pick you up at four," I say.

Kat shakes her head.

"Chelsea and me might go out. I'll text you if I need a ride."

"You can go ahead and text me either way," I say, but I'm not sure she hears me because the door slams right on the word "way."

I drive out of the parking lot, my right foot light as a feather as I sing what I can remember from my last night's homework to Samuel in the backset. It's not a bad way to study.

I'm taking classes in Machining Technology. I'm hoping eventually to get an FAA certificate and work on planes. That would be great. But anything working with my hands would be fine. I just want a job. If I could bring in some money, then Kat can quit her job and become the kind of mom that bakes cookies, and we can afford to start giving Samuel better things like new clothes instead of the ones we now pick up secondhand.

I park a million miles away because campus parking permits are practically like a second tuition. Then I waddle across campus, a bag on each shoulder, and Samuel strapped to my belly with one of those sling things that make you look pregnant.

My first day of classes I was scared. I hadn't been in a classroom for fifteen years and that's if my junior and senior years of high school counted which maybe they didn't since I spent almost as much time skipping classes as I did attending them. That was another worry. My grades were crappy in high school, but was that because of all the sloughing or was it because I was just plain dumb? Plus, at the time the semester started I was only twenty days sober and it didn't help that the place was crawling with these ridiculously hot young chicks wearing ridiculously hot young clothes. On the second day of classes I purposefully left out my contact lenses so I wouldn't be able to see them. But if anything that made it worse since my imagination was left to play freely with the blurry outlines I was presented with. Besides, I couldn't see the board from the back row which is where I felt I needed to sit what with Samuel and the possibility of the occasional crying issue or dirty diaper.

My first class of the day is a required composition class. In order to get us to think about purpose and audience we are doing group work where we are supposed to come up with an ad that will rejuvinate the Post-It note market in the face of cellphones and text-messaging and all that. My idea is to have some sort of supermodel come on screen covered in nothing but Post-Its. One-by-one people from all walks of life will come by and pluck one off her. There's no sound or anything and just as the audience at home is about to freak out it fades to black and a message of something like "This is not your father's Post-It" comes up. I mean sex sells and we're trying to inject some oomph into a basically dying thing. But I don't say anything. I'm the oldest one in the class by probably ten years and I don't want to come across as the old pervert. So I just sit bouncing Samuel on my leg and listen as my group comes up with an incredibly boring ad about how Post-Its help some guy get organized and then promoted at the office.

The next class is Machine Technology I. So far it's all been stuff out of a textbook with video examples. But I can see on the syllabus that in a week or two we are going to be in the shop and this raises a question about Samuel. I mean most of my classes are going to have a heavy hands-on component. Which means as much as I like the vision of Samuel right there next to me in a mini welder's shield I'm going to have to look into baby sitting. The campus has a center for that but so far I haven't been able to bring myself to go and check it out. I keep picturing my kid having to play with a toy that some other kid has slobbered all over.

Classes done, the afternoon stretches before us. My only goal is to avoid the TV which looms like 55" of high def hell. TV is almost a guarantee of alcohol and alcohol could pretty quickly lead to more alcohol and one thing I know about myself now is that the end of an equation with alcohol in it is not somewhere I want to go.

So I look for something to clean. I vacuumed two days ago. Cleaned the bathroom the day before that. I run my finger along the shelf of a bookcase that houses DVDs, a few old magazines plus the picture of me, Kat and Samuel at the hospital. But my finger comes up clean.

I clean the kitchen every night but I realize I've never actually cleaned the inside of the refrigerator. So I take all the contents out and line them up on the counter.

Right away I see this was maybe kind of a mistake. There are three beers in the back. Two PBR's and a Heineken. I open the freezer drawer and see an almost full bottle of vodka. When I take the cereal boxes down to wipe off the top of the fridge I find a bottle of wine hiding behind them. I remember, or rather had just tried to keep myself from thinking about, the big bottle of Southern Comfort under the house.

"This," I say to Samuel. "Is what is known as temptation."

Kat would never know. Or more to the point these days, she wouldn't care. I never came out and told Kat I'd quit drinking. I felt like if I told her I would be creating expectations and my whole life my relationship to expectations has not been a good one. So I kept the no drinking thing to myself. Given how much we fought about it in the past I figured Kat would eventually notice something was up. But going on four months and she hasn't said anything.

I set Samuel's carrier on the kitchen table. My hands are shaking as I 409 the shelves and the inside of the crisper and that little butter holder place. I don't throw out the booze. I get through it by making it a lesson for Samuel. I tell him the name of every damn thing I put in that refrigerator including the stuff I throw out like an expired yogurt and an empty bottle of mayonnaise that someone scraped clean and then put back anyway.

"When you finish something you throw it out," I say to Samuel and drop the jar in the trashcan.

When I'm done and close the refrigerator door I hear that tiny little suction sound it makes when it closes all the way. I breathe deep and lean my forehead against the cool surface of the door. Then I get online and search for a recipe for tonight's dinner. I find one for beef stroganoff which looks good. Samuel and I drive to the grocery store for the ingredients—not Alpha Beta but a bigger one closer to us.

I had sort of hoped Kat would call while we were out so I could swing by the mall and pick her up. But no dice. By the time we get home it is close to five. I go ahead and make dinner. When it's done I give Samuel his bottle and put him to bed before eating a plate of the stroganoff. By the time I've put the leftovers in the fridge and cleaned up it is approaching eight o'clock. I double-check my phone. No messages. No missed calls.

I go back to the bookshelf and see what's there that doesn't involve TV. Mainly there are a whole bunch of books on CD that Kat has been checking out from the library and when I check the date on a couple of them I see they are overdue. They are self help books with titles like *201 Life Changing Moves that are Right in Front of Your Eyes* or *The Fallacy of Imperfection* or *Finding Your Own Estuary*. I turn off all the lights except for the one in the hall. I put in a disc called *Not Being Afraid of Being You*. I don't understand much of it but I like the voice that's reading. It's a man's voice, soft yet firm, so I stretch out on the floor and listen to words like "authenticity" and "efficacy" bounce around on the ceiling.

I sort of half fall asleep until headlights sweep across the living room and the gravel crunches outside. I look at the clock on the cable box. 10:35.

Kat comes in and drops her bag on the floor. She kicks off her shoes—one, two—in a way so that they do a neat little flip in the air like maybe they were members of some shoe circus.

"Work good?" I say.

"No. It was shit of course," she says. But even though that's what she said I can tell she's in a good mood. Something I haven't seen her in in a long time. I go over and give her a kiss. She kisses me back. I taste something. I can't tell what, but it's definitely stronger than a mudslide.

"Do we have anything to drink?" she says.

"I don't know," I say. "Some beer in the fridge. Maybe some vodka."

"Vodka? Where?"

"In the freezer."

I go into the living room and sit down in the recliner and

watch Kat make her drink. She takes a tall glass, puts a liberal pour of vodka into it. She throws in some ice cubes and a splash of orange juice. The she comes over to me and sits on the recliner's armrest.

"Want some?" she says.

I shake my head.

"No, not right now," I say.

Kat shrugs and takes a long drink from the glass. She stays on the armrest and with the drink in one hand sort of twirls my hair with the other. We sit like that for ten minutes or so in the near dark while Kat finishes her drink. When it's gone, and she's crunched an ice cube, she leans over to set the glass down on the carpet but almost topples over onto the floor herself except that she reaches for me and I'm able to catch her and I pull her back up with one arm. She laughs. Then she kisses me and with a free hand grabs my crotch.

It's the first time we've had sex since Samuel. It is sort of awkward at first, then it gets good, then it gets real good. Afterwards we lay in bed side by side, breathing heavy and staring at the ceiling.

"Let's go to Village Inn," she says.

"What do you want at Village Inn?" I say. "I can make you anything they've got."

"Awww. C'mon. That's not the point. I don't know what I want," she says. "What I want is to look at a whole bunch of pictures of food. Then, when I do decide, I want to point and have it look exactly like it did in the picture when it arrives in front of me."

We pack up Samuel, who doesn't even stir from his sleep, and go to Village Inn where we look at pictures of food. When the waitress comes Kat points to chicken-fried steak and eggs. I point to a piece of French silk pie.

We eat more or less in silence, Samuel zonked out on the booth next to me. The pie is good but in almost the same amount of time it takes me to eat it Kat devours her entire meal, even mopping up the last of the egg yolk and ketchup with the edge of a triangle of toast.

On the way home, when we pass 7th Street, Kat says, "Oh, let's go by the store. The A.B."

I maneuver the car back toward 7th and we drive out to the Alpha Beta. It's after one o'clock in the morning. The store is closed, the parking lot little envelopes of light and shadow from the parking lamps overhead. I park in the back, back where Kat used to, so we can take in the whole thing.

"Remember?" Kat says.

"Sure," I say.

"Tell me one thing specifically."

"Like the names of the post-soviet states?"

"No. Something about me. Back then. But how many are there?"

"There were fifteen according to your textbook."

"Name them."

"Armenia, Georgia, Moldova, Russia, Ukraine, Azerbaijan—my favorite."

"Keep going."

"Lithuania, Kyrgystan, Belarus. Estonia. Latvia. Uzbekistan."

"That's twelve," Kat said who'd been holding up fingers.

"OK," I said. "Then how about I remember I couldn't believe you would even talk to me let alone go out with me. How you were the prettiest thing I'd ever seen. You even had pretty skin. Pretty ears. Who has pretty ears? But you did."

Kat nods.

"You needed me," she says.

By the time we get home I am exhausted. I put Samuel in his crib and get in bed. Kat wants to take a shower. As I listen to her in the water I think "sprinkler." Was that just yesterday? Amazing, I think. Life. I remember that seeming very profound as I fell asleep.

When I woke up the next morning Kat wasn't beside me. I gave Samuel's toe a wiggle and went out to the living room where there was a note on the kitchen table. In some ways the note explained everything, but of course in other ways it explained nothing. It was written on a piece of paper torn out from one of the spiral notebooks I used for school. While I read the note those little fringe things that run along the side of the paper stuck to my fingers, my shirt and by the time I'd read the note twice and then three times the little things were everywhere. I found them for a long time after and in places I never would have expected.

I went outside. I don't know why. I suppose I had some image in my mind of her just pulling out of the drive, or just barely down the street, somewhere where I could run after her, flag her down, make her stop. But she was gone.

The self-help CD last night said that one should never "be ashamed of seeking solace." So I went inside to get my keys. It was the only solace I knew other than Samuel and Kat. It wasn't until I came back out and found nothing to put the keys in that I noticed. She'd taken Deep Blue. Of course. Made sense. Samuel and I would need the car. I wasn't sure you could even put a carseat on a motorcycle. Or if you could that you'd want to.

So instead of firing up Deep Blue I went around to the side of the house and turned on Zones 1 and 2 simultaneously. As I stood watching my sprinklers watering dirt, I wasn't sure anymore that the sod was even necessary. It'd be plenty nice just to have this to turn on whenever you wanted. Whenever you needed to. The way the water and sun turned the air into a jewel. The way the sound of the ten sprinkler heads was nothing short of a lullaby. Maybe I'd put the grass in later, when Samuel was older and in need of a place to run, to throw, to hit a ball with a bat. On the other hand, I'd probably be in contention for Father of the Year if I gave my son an expanse of mud this big to play in.

But however the turn of things went it would be without Kat. Wherever she was off to, I hoped it got her back close to that girl I first met. The one with a tiny red car, a backseat of books, a university, a future. I was betting she would. Deep

Blue was a great bike. I knew the fat back tire would hold true while the front one pointed forward, putting away the miles, heading toward some future or another. Just not this one.

LOVE LETTER, OR LEPIDOPTERY

(Camouflage Vladimir Nabokov, *Transparent Things*)

Your first tattoo. Blocks of blackness on a white tablet.
Your skin a kind of Esperanto between how others read it and
how you do. I still look for tattoos because of you. Arms, necks,
breasts, legs, backs, chests, fingers, even lips. Eyelids. Each one
a paperback blurb promising things nothing could actually deliver. Love. Peace. Honor. God. Wisdom. Self.

I sometimes, I often, look back and see I was really just a
tourist. You were bilingual. Living in a way I never could. You
moved, or rather wiggled, between presence and absence, the
easy and the incalculable. You knew when the seduction of the
past was more desirable than the erotic silkiness of the future.
And vice versa. You knew that between the surface and the
innards is the heart.

I was about holding on. Stability. Stasis. A word I always
heard the Siren's call of self-esteem behind. Even if it meant
pretending sometimes.

Yet here we are. In our way. The cobwebbery of old age.
There's a library of you, memories I can pull randomly from any
of the shelves in my mind. By the way, you were right. I see that

now. I can see the consolation in the glass white of abstraction. It took me all this time to realize how much more preferable it is to the dog-fogged silhouette of the here and now.

SCHOOL
(Camouflage Paul Auster, *City of Glass*)

They're perched like sphinxes on the front steps of the school. One opens a V between his legs and dribbles a long stream of saliva. It is football brown and mentholated. Juice from an odd fruit.

It's chew this year, just as it was cigarettes last. It has always been that way. What's cool. Cords one year, jeans the next. One year you eat cafeteria food, the next you bring your own. It's not calculated. No one holds a summit and decides to go from white briefs to checkered boxers. They just do. Its glassy invisibility is cool's magic. A mute language impossible to decipher. By the time it trickles down to you it's too late. You've already bought your briefs, your cords, your wheel of lunch tickets.

They are a necessary tyranny. Part heroes, part proxies, part warnings. On the front grass, the other students eat lunch. P.B. and Js, soft-boiled eggs, chips inside two ounce Mylar balloons. The decadent unreality of Twinkies, Ho-Hos and Ding Dongs. The five on the steps no longer eat lunch. Eating is what animals do. They are gods. Gods do not eat.

Instead, like watermelon seeds, they spit out an intermittent word or two. They talk math. Ms. Hamilton, the algebra teacher. They talk about her fucking. How she likes to do it. They want to know real sex. Adult sex. Not movie sex or what they've done on couches or car seats wrestling zippers, pawing at buttons. There was the one unforgettable day when they saw her run across the street to her car, her milky-blue dress transparent with sunlight. Ms. Hamilton wears her hair in an innocent ponytail, but has a body that belongs to what their fathers still call "girlie magazines." To bring her closer, to knock her down a peg, they tried testing her first name on their tongues. But when they spoke that small word it grew bigger than them. Now "Ms. Hamilton" suffices. They've been taught a lesson. How strange the relationship of language to the world.

Talk is safer when it's about girls their own age. For every other boy, girls are a labyrinth. To these five they are a menu. A constantly amended ranking of appetizers, entrees, sides and desserts. But these girls are lucky. They aren't faceless. Or more to the point, bodiless. So many others in the school are.

The bell rings. Instead of class they drive to a convenience store. Three in the back, one calling "shotgun." They shoplift with methods so ingrained they sometimes forget they are stealing. They go to the park, smoke pot, listen to music spun from silvery discs. The driver lies down on the hood. They eat Snickers, Sprees, Salted Nut Rolls, Nerds.

When the sun dips and clouds begin pooling, it's late enough to go home. Home, where they're seventeen. Where they are addressed by pseudonyms like "Junior," "Chucky Boy," and "Sweet-Ums." As they cross the threshold from the real world to home, they have to refashion facades by trying to remember themselves as they had been before.

TREE

(Camouflage Diane Williams, *Excitability: Selected Stories 1986-1996*)

From where I'm sitting I only catch a glimpse of the woman jogging before she disappears behind the plum tree. An iridescent ribbon of sunlight falls across the chair where I am reading. Before the jogger, I was contemplating going upstairs and changing into daytime clothes.

It's the time of year when small plums jewel the south side of the tree. They're about the size of golf balls. Their skin is a lacquered fuchsia. I don't eat the fruit, but my wife enjoys it.

I take my drink to the window and look out. The woman is already far down the next block. I want to know how attractive she is. All I saw was a black jogging outfit with neon green stripes that made her look as sleek as a seal. I want to know what she looks like. Not her clothes. Her. This not knowing is a tiny piece of blindness in my soul. No matter how much I wish it wouldn't, my mind won't rest until it fills that outfit in one way or another. It's already running through short scenarios of coincidence and providence.

The north side of the tree is unornamented and the branches

are the ember black they remain all year. It looks like the tree was drawn in Japanese ink. It is my favorite part of the house. My wife wants to cut the branches off or maybe even cut the whole tree down. It's a hazard she says.

In my imagination the woman jogs up to the front porch and without knocking comes inside. She opens my robe and gives me the tenderest of caresses. She keeps the suit on until the very last minute. When she takes it off, it's like she's peeling a skin. Afterwards we will embrace—each other and the happy afternoon.

The problem is the tree is dying from the inside. Still, I try. Every spring I stop by the hardware store for sharp tubes of elixir.

I go home and stab the tree many, many times.

CIGARETTES

(Camouflage Don DeLillo, *Mao II*, Chapter Two)

He watches as a splashy white car sweeps the dark window, its headlights bent stalks reflecting off the glass. The thing was about to happen. What had been theory, plan, make-believe is now a shadow taking on dimension. His hands grope for the relief of cigarettes.

A large man comes into the room and takes the desk chair, flipping it around to face the rest of the room. There's only one other place to sit so he takes the bed. He feels awkward with one foot anchored to the floor the other floating freely as he rests a thigh on the mattress in order to face the man. Power no matter how small a measure you can take.

The two are silent for what feels like a long time. He wants to say something but his mind stutters against the emptiness of monochrome reality. His tongue has become a tourist. Finally he gets enough words together to offer the man a glass of the gas station wine he's been drinking. The man takes a sip and begins to speak. The man speaks in an unsettling whisper. An intimate whisper. Like he is telling him private things. They aren't private things. They are things they both already know.

He nods anyway to indicate he is paying attention and when the time comes he goes to the closet and retrieves a thick box labeled "Shoes" in red marker.

The man looks inside, nods, and opens two of the baggies. The man insists he take some with him. He shouldn't. He's already taken two earlier in the evening and another just before the man arrived. But there is no other way. They take it at the same time, washing it down with wine, and before long the room goes predictably remote, foreign and soft. He goes to the window and looks out. His eyes want fresh air. He knows it's paranoid phantasm but quickly closes the shades after seeing a mirage of dozens of telephoto lenses winking in the parking lot.

As he walks back to his spot on the bed he notices the painting above the headboard is cut. It is a bland painting of a horse but is an actual oil stretched out on real canvas. The horse has a horizontal slit down the length of its side. How did he not notice that before in the eight hours he'd spent in the room? Could the man have done it while he was occupied with the window? Was it a warning? A threat? He hadn't seen the man move from the chair since taking the drug, just staring at the orange and brown pattern of the comforter on the bed. The whole room smells like the comforter, even with the cigarette smoke. He sees the gun in the armpit holster beneath the man's jacket. He assumes there is at least one more man in a car outside. Probably one in the hallway with an ear cocked towards the door. He is struck by the thin difference between concealment and disappearance.

As if reading his mind, the man speaks.

"Why'd you pick this dump anyway?" the man says.

"I'll tell you the truth," he answers. "I have no idea where we are."

SHADES

(Camouflage Homer, *The Odyssey*, Book Eleven)

There is a place I take you where roller-skating handmaids twirl with food-stacked trays braced on fingertips. They deliver sundaes to our car window already softened by the night's summering heat. It is a ceremony, and like all ceremonies it is a kind of protection. We experience nostalgia at a place that's only been here two years. We pretend to a past that is not our past. Under the half-moon we can go so far as to pretend instead of Accords and Corollas it is beastly Thunderbirds and Fairlanes moored to the intercom stands. Nickel hubcaps and chrome fins, long vinyl bench seats as smooth as ice. Sawed-off mufflers, play thick in the ears, instead of the quiet whine of efficiency.

There were plenty of places, patiently waiting our return, where we had actually gone as youths.

But there was enough of that at home. An eye-mask my only armor against the impalpable shadows. I lie in bed like a blind man buckled under blankets and wait. For how they make me feel, you would think they were flaming devils of torture. But they are faint images of the past, whispers blown together, that sneak through untouched and carve at my soul.

HANDS

(Camouflage Georges Perec, *A Void*)

I'm good with my hands. I got tools, a blow torch, all sorts of scraping things and sharp razors. In addition to wood that is locally around, I got a stash of bamboo I bought from a catalog. Isn't a thing I can't build. But no girl thinks of that.

Good hands will bring a job as good as my pa-pa's. Anybody'd do proud having four rooms and an island to cook on. If I find a girl and cash is short, I can build us bonus stuff. Form an illusion of living in a rich world.

But girls can't look past football and trucks. I took on both. Got hit so hard in football, grass almost took my pants off. I got a truck, and it's a loyal companion. But what it is not is mint. Or big. It's a flaking gray light-duty from '98. A jalopy. Looks mighty poor against a half-ton 350 with a tough V8. It's how things work in this town. To pitch your woo you gotta bait a girl into your truck. Kind of a cryptic ritual with all sorts of moving parts I know nothing about on account of I'm too shy to chum.

Grown boys and girls playing with trucks is about par for this town. This town is mud. With a truck you might can ward off monotony. Got a shot, anyway. Without it, say howdy-hi to nothing but a continuous, undying grind.

Tonight I go to Community Faith and its churchyard. Out back is lots of land with stout oaks and thick, lush grass thanks to abundant plots from folks that's now stiff. All of us kids go 'round it on Friday and Saturday nights, Thursdays too, from about junior high on. Not cuz it's spooky or dramatic. Just that it's our only public park. It's to drink at. Mostly drinking. But marijuana too, obviously. Tonight I'm working at my old man's whisky. Not a worry at all. I won't go back until past dawn and pa's no risk mornings—too raw and vacant to think of hurting a fly.

Our churchyard has two big things. It's got a tin sign, so way back it's hard to find, sunk down among roots and dirt indicating a sighting and abduction via UFO transmission in 1953. Kinda odd for a church, I think, or possibly not so much now that I think about it. Yard also has a gigantic tomb for a family important to founding this town. Why you'd want to mark that with a bunch of fancy calligraphy cut into a rock, who knows. Rumors say it had an actual diamond on it, big as a mixing bowl. Naturally it got took.

Tonight I got no company. Only soul around. Ha-ha. Prom night. I was going too. But Sarah Brooks didn't want yours truly. I'm a discard—got an actual card from Sarah Brooks with my dismissal on it. Just a short paragraph. Hurtfully short but just as bad, damn ink did a slow vanishing act midway through. First pink ink, which at halfway runs out, so now it turns black. Sarah Brooks couldn't worry about doing it again and fixing it right. It's just civil. A singular color is all I ask.

Truck's radio is on. A station from a county past ours just so I'm away from this town. Partially, anyway. Thinking about Sarah Brooks was bad. My blood starts dancing. Soon my body is throbbing. I put a hand in my pants and start pacing up and down my rapidly hard cock. I'm picturing Sarah Brooks in flimsy satin, with fancy bows. Laying down and glowing on a giant rug. Just for that ink thing, I put it in backdoor as an animal would. I orgasm, jizz oozing down my fist, my cum mirroring bright moonlight.

I calm down, dozing a bit. I look toward town and its way off horizon shows a first flash of dawn. A ghost of purplish crimson. A vision. I zip-up and wish Sarah Brooks into my truck so us pair could look out at what's starting. That's all. Just watch. I'd swap it for all that stuff on a rug rubbish quick as a blink. In my mind I'm apologizing hard. A mind can play hocus-pocus with imaginings.

As an illustration. That big divot dug out of that humungous tomb? No way it was an actual diamond. Probably just amazingly stunning glass. Still, look down into that cavity at night and word of honor you'll find a glowing light, a diamond shadow that got stuck high and dry.

THE PHANTOM PUNCH

When Joel was seven years old he wanted to be a hobo. He'd read about hoboes in a book. How they "rode the rails" and slept under the stars and had a secret code of squiggles which they scratched onto the sides of barns and fences to tell other hoboes about the people who lived there. The book even had a drawing of one—a little guy with a potbelly and a checkerboard kerchief tied to a stick. That night at the dinner table Joel announced that that was the life for him.

On Saturday, Joel's father took him to Pioneer Park, a park he'd never been to on a side of town he'd never seen. Although it was Saturday the swing set sat unused. Same for the big metal slide that twisted in a wide, inviting S. On the merry-go-round was a man dressed in too many clothes for the early summer weather. He lay crumpled, fetal, as the flat disk spun him in a slow and indifferent circle. There were similar men, and as far as Joel could tell they were all men, scattered throughout the park—lying on the grass, lying on picnic benches. One was sitting in a nest of blankets with his back against a tree. Nobody was standing.

"Those are hoboes," his father said.

They stood for a few minutes in silence and then his father

lead him back to the car.

When Joel was ten he saw a boxing movie on TV. It was about some guy who improbably goes into boxing to win money for his saintly wife and sickly son. It made a big impression; probably in no small part because the main character, the hero, was named Joel too. He talked about the movie for weeks.

When October came around his father suggested Joel should be a boxer for Halloween. His father almost always dictated his choice of Halloween costume. It wasn't that he wasn't allowed to choose for himself. It was just that his own ideas could never match his father's in terms of imagination and enthusiasm, or the unstated fact that money would be no object in seeing the vision came true.

So Joel was a boxer. His mother sewed his name on the back of his bathrobe, the one he wore on Christmas morning and maybe one or two other times a year when he was sick. On the toy aisle of a store his father found him a pair of ridiculously oversized boxing gloves—two fat pillows really, stuck like giant marshmallows at the end of his stick-like arms. Halloween night his father sat him down at his mother's vanity and applied various make-ups to his face. He gave Joel a black eye. With some flesh colored putty to make it look swollen and a couple of band-aids, his father gave him a broken nose. His father created a deep bruise that covered an entire cheek, a cut and bleeding eyebrow, a blacked-out missing tooth. The joke, his father told him, as Joel looked at himself in the mirror, was to tell people "You should see the other guy."

When he was fourteen Joel and his friends were allowed to make a weekly excursion to the mall—without parents. There they were free, wholly untethered from home. In truth, the mall had to be smaller in total area than the nine block neighborhood radius they'd been allowed on their bicycles since age seven. But it felt huge. There were bright lights, and food that for the first time in your life you bought yourself, and every store window offered up a different possibility of a potential you.

In one window, a shoe store where the employees wore referee shirts—as if they were there to enforce some set of mystery rules that no one else knew rather than to sell footwear—there was a poster of Muhammad Ali. A famous one. Maybe *the* famous one. The one where he's just knocked down Sonny Liston, who for all you can tell is dead on the canvas. Ali is standing over him, towering, one fist cocked, with an expression on his face that said so much to Joel about so many things that he had to have it.

The poster went up over his bed, a space that had previously been occupied by a Star Wars poster of a TIE Fighter in hot pursuit of an X-Wing. His father didn't say anything about the Ali poster but he obviously took note, because just a few weeks later he announced he'd gotten tickets to a night of amateur youth boxing matches.

Like the hobo park, the fights were on the westside of town in an old Kiwanis gymnasium. Like the park almost all in attendance were men. Like the park they were overwhelmingly Mexican. Unlike the hoboes however, the boxers were lean and sleek, bouncing as if barely able to contain the strength and energy constrained in their compact bodies. But like the park the scene scared Joel a little bit, maybe even a lot, even if he couldn't quite name why.

Joel had never seen two people hit each other before. Had never seen violence of any sort in real life. He'd seen lots of violence on TV and in movies of course. But that was mainly just visual; it was the look of violence, the appearance of it. What struck him here was the sound. It wasn't a big sound, but it went deep in a way that no sound effects guy slapping a melon or a ham in a recording studio was ever going to get close to.

His father didn't say much during the fights, just occasionally commented on a good punch or made a prediction about who he thought would win as the boxers stood through their introductions. But the message was plain. This excursion was another lesson in "reality," to bring Joel back down to earth by showing him the world and reminding him of his place in it.

Outside the arena, several card tables were set out advertising boxing lessons. When the bouts were over, and he and his father were heading for the exit, Joel went over and signed up for one.

He was one of three white kids at the gym and the other two were so much older than Joel it was as much of a gulf as skin color. There was one African-American, one Asian-American. Everyone else was Mexican.

Being a "minority" was a whole new experience for Joel. Sometimes he felt incredibly self-conscious like he was just one giant walking zit. But most of the time Joel felt invisible, as if he literally was "white" and nobody could do anything other than look through him.

There were probably a half dozen or so trainers in the gym at any given time, but it was hard to tell because the gym was not only a place to workout and box—it was a place to socialize. All kinds of men loitered around. There were old men scratching lottery cards with quarters, damp stubs of cigars in their mouths. There were young men in expensive looking suits and flashing expensive looking watches. There were even little kids running all over and pestering anyone who would listen for loose change to feed the vending machines out by the check-in desk. So the gym was loud. Several of the boxers would often bring boom-boxes and play them simultaneously, the strange music joining the general noise of conversation and laughter, the clang of weights, the whistle and snap of jump ropes—all echoing, amplified in the stark acoustics of the wide, high-ceilinged room.

His instruction was, to say the least, informal. When Joel arrived at his appointed time someone who was hanging out by the main desk would detach himself from it for long enough to point him to some exercise, which he would do, until someone came by and pointed him to something else.

Joel enjoyed the exercises though. Straightforward and methodical, they offered a new kind of satisfaction he hadn't experienced before. But what he really wanted was a chance at the speed bag. There were two in the gym—small pear-shaped pieces of stuffed leather that you punched in a rhythm of rights and lefts until the bag was nothing but a blur, the only evidence of its existence the sound of it slapping against the top of the support. The bags were off toward the back of the gym but they were essentially its center. The older boys stood around them, kidding with each other and waiting for their turn. Often shouting and sometimes even a small fight broke out when someone thought someone else was hogging a bag.

"It's good for nothing but show," one of the trainers said to Joel when he asked about giving it a try. "That's why they call it a peanut bag. You waste your time on that and that's what you become, a cacahuate."

Instead of the speed bag Joel was most often put on the heavy bag. A long, fat cylinder that hung down from the ceiling on a chain, dull and dense like a dead body. When he punched it an electric current shot up from his wrists and into his shoulders where the ache would live for days.

His lessons were at three o'clock, Tuesdays and Thursdays, which meant his mother drove him, dropping him off, saying something about shopping and that she'd be back at five. Joel was never sure exactly where she went shopping during these hours, nor did the nameless shopping bags piled in the backseat offer any clues.

They rarely made it home before 5:30 by which time his father would be sitting in the living room with a cocktail. His father favored real dad-type drinks—Martinis, Manhattans, Old-fashions. Drinks that allowed for the elaborate rituals of shakers and garnishes, with any luck a muddler.

"Wax on, wax off today?" his father would say or some such jibe that took Joel's training down to the level of something like piano lessons, which it probably was really, but the way his father said it made it seem even sillier than sitting on a wooden bench, poking at fake ivory keys while an egg-timer measured the minutes to your freedom.

"Aaaaaaaadrian," his father would bellow, more Brando than Stallone, as he made himself a second drink.

The usual coda to this was his father walking over to Joel, putting an arm around him and saying, "Just kidding, champ. I'll bet you're doing great down there."

But it was hard for Joel to measure his progress at the gym, or exactly what that progress would even look like. He was, however, unmistakably different at home. He ate constantly, insatiable in a way that made him feel like some monster run amok only instead of a city he was laying waste to the kitchen. To help appease him his mother took to buying gallons of milk and writing his name on them with black marker so that he could drink straight from the jug as he prowled for something more substantial. He ate anything that presented itself— crackers, pickles, peanut butter straight from the jar. His favorite was instant ramen. He didn't bother to take the time to cook it. He just tore open the cellophane and sat on the sofa sprinkling the flavor packet onto each brick of dehydrated noodles, then eating it like a bear with a claw full of honeycomb.

His body was different too. He was aware of it in a way he hadn't been before. Whether he was taking a shower or tying his shoes or just sprawled out on his bed staring at the ceiling, he was filled with a new sense of the physical space he took up in the world. Sometimes he would pick something up—a basketball, a schoolbook—something he'd held a thousand times before and all at once it felt light, toy-like, insubstantial in a way that made him smile and sometimes even laugh.

But he also felt unbelievably tired. All the time. Especially during the day, much more so than at night. Sleep came anywhere, anytime. He might fall asleep on the couch and then wake up only to move to his bedroom and fall asleep again. Basically he slept whenever he wasn't eating and in that way it was a kind of hibernation. The sleep in these naps was light though, there was always one part of his brain in the outside world—

he was half aware of the television, his stereo, the comings and goings of his parents, all of which leaked into his dreams. But those things didn't make his dreams feel more real. Instead, when he woke-up, the world felt more dreamlike.

Slowly, and Joel had no idea if this had been planned or things had just happened this way, instead of a randomly rotating cast of trainers, his sessions at the gym started to funnel down to the purview of just two— Juan Manuel and Juan Carlos who began not just to train him but to coach him as well.

One afternoon Joel was at the heavy bag, his routine warm-up, when Juan Manuel came over to him, took him by the shoulders and turned Joel around to face him.

"No," he said. "Today is sparring."

Juan Manuel surely saw the look of terror in Joel's face to which he said with a shrug, "Boxing is simple. You hit. You get hit."

The two of them went up front to the equipment room where Juan Manuel held up a jockstrap.

"You got one of these?" he said.

Joel shook his head.

Juan Manuel threw it to him.

"Buy one," he said. "And one of these too." He tossed him a cup. "Extra-Large, right?" he said and laughed.

The jockstrap and cup felt weird and uncomfortable but he put them on and went back outside to the gym.

There were two rings in the gym. One was reserved, in an unspoken way, for the special fighters. He saw Juan Manuel at the other one waving him over.

He felt like he was sleepwalking as Juan Manuel rattled off some instructions while taping his wrists so tightly it hurt. When he was finished taping he slipped gloves over Joel's mummified hands and tied them tight. The gloves were hard, harder than Joel had imagined, maybe even harder than hands, he thought. The final pieces of equipment were a mouthpiece and protective headgear that sat wobbly on his head even after it was secured in place by a Velcro strap under his chin.

Juan Manuel parted the ropes and Joel stepped through them into the ring. The headgear felt like a space helmet, so much so that he was still looking around trying to orient himself when his sparring partner came over and gave him a left hook to his right temple. He could hear Juan Manuel's voice ringside and he wanted to hear what he was saying, to know what to do, but all he could think about was how weird the punch had felt. It hurt. There was no doubt about that. He didn't know it then but he would down a handful of aspirin that night and would still have trouble sleeping because of the dull ache in his head. But it hadn't hurt in the way he thought it would.

The bulbous headgear made everything seem on a slight delay, like it wasn't happening to you but to some identical twin of yours which you felt a split-second later. It was that sensation of being himself and yet not himself that calmed Joel down, let him locate his opponent, and start to box.

When the session was over, one untimed round, Joel climbed back through the ropes, off the elevated ring and back to the gym floor. Juan Manuel took off his headgear pulled out the mouthpiece, reaching into his mouth with what felt like his whole hand as if Joel was a horse that was having its age checked. Juan Manuel gave Joel a squirt of water from a bottle

"You'll get better," he said and proceeded to remove the gloves.

Dinner was Joel's father's favorite time of the day. With the yellow flush-mount light shining down, the table became his private stage. He talked almost non-stop. It was almost like a magic act. The food disappeared off his plate but you never noticed him taking a bite. Instead he told jokes, recapped articles he'd read, relayed a bit of trivia he'd heard on the radio, held-forth with long polemics on politics and if nothing new offered itself up he'd simply circle back to something old. The story about accidentally setting fire to his high school baseball field that they'd heard a thousand times, the one about the cherry bomb, the one about old Mr. Miller and his cane, Mrs. Knutson and her purse, the one about the graveyard.

But lately a new topic had introduced itself into the monolog. The idea of relocating his job. Joel's father was an engineer with a private firm that dealt mostly in government military contracts with the Air Force base about an hour southwest of the city. Joel's father was doing well there. Very well as far as Joel could tell. A year didn't go by that didn't see his father announcing a raise and every few months a bonus usually came along as well. So this desire to relocate was puzzling. Perhaps the base was closing and the firm was downsizing. Perhaps his father had done something wrong and was about to be fired. But if there was something wrong you couldn't tell it from the cheerful demeanor of his father as he divulged the latest candidate.

"So I sent out a tentative call to BTM," he'd say. "I was just looking around and saw that Dirk Ford, this guy who used to be here, works there now. I mean I didn't know him really well but I figured it couldn't hurt."

"And where is BTM?" his mother asked.

"Kentucky," his father said. "Louisville. Wouldn't that be great? You know, horses and everything? The economy out there is booming. Great opportunities but nobody ever thinks Kentucky. Which is why this is so great. It's ours for the taking."

This was at least the seventh or eighth place that had been held up as a possible destination. The first two times—North Carolina and then a couple of weeks later San Diego—Joel had told his friends he was going to be moving. It made him feel special somehow. Like he was above everything and everybody now, even the teachers, because he wasn't really there anymore. But when both of those turned out to be nothing more than wishful thinking on the part of his father he stopped telling his friends about these "prospects" because surely, if Joel didn't believe in them himself, how could he expect anyone else to.

"Abraham Lincoln is from Kentucky," Joel's father said. "Illinois may claim they're the 'Land of Lincoln' but he was born in Hardin County, Kentucky. Know who else is a Kentuckian? John T. Thompson. Know who that is, Joel?"

"No idea."

"Ha! Of course not. But I bet you would if I told you the nickname of the thing he invented. The Thompson Machine Gun? Aka the 'Tommy Gun'?"

"Great, Dad," Joel said and went back to his food while his father continued on as a one-man Chamber of Commerce for the state of Kentucky.

He sparred once a week at the gym and as he got better it increased to twice a week. Sometimes he was even put in the "good" ring. The sense of distance, the slight out-of-body quality he felt in the ring, made Joel treat his opponents' blows as simply small punishments for miscalculations on his part, like losing a pawn in chess, or in the case of a well-placed upper-cut, maybe a rook.

It was this strategic approach that earned him, for the first time in his life, a nickname. One day when he was sparring Juan Carlos, who was coaching him through the match, said loudly but to no one in particular, "Look at him in there. Jabbing away. Like a *viejecita* in the kitchen. Jabber, jabber, jabber."

And so at the gym he became "Jabber." Which was ironic because at school he was quiet and shy. But no one else at school ever went to the westside of town. No one else traded punches on a regular basis with other males sometimes two or three years older than him. True, nobody ever actually saw him boxing. But the fact that it went unseen, the fact that he only ever talked about it briefly to his friends and let them spread and embellish it, only enhanced the mystique. Joel walked the halls with as much clout as any of the other jocks at school, even the football players, which is surely why Susanna Mitchum came up to him at his locker one day between 5th and 6th periods. By the time she left for 6th it had been decided, Joel wasn't sure by which of them, that they go out that Saturday.

Susanna was a senior. Blond, pretty, she'd been a cheerleader for two years before quitting because she wanted to concentrate on volleyball in hopes of getting a scholarship. "Plus volleyball is just more interesting, you know?" she would later tell Joel. "I mean you can only shake pom-poms for so long."

Joel was a sophomore. A young one too, still only fifteen. So for their date Susanna had to pick him up. She pulled to the curb in a boat of a car that had to be older than either one of them. Probably older than both of them combined. It had bench seats, over-sized headlights and push button door handles attached to heavy doors that practically closed on you if you weren't quick about getting all of your parts inside.

"My father's," Susanna explained. "We have two other cars that nobody drives either. They just sit in the garage with flat tires. He's like that with everything. Can't throw anything away. But I guess in this case, lucky me!"

They went for burgers and a movie. At the end of the evening Susanna gave Joel a peck on the cheek. Everything was straight out of Frank Capra except the goodnight kiss was on Joel's doorstep not hers.

After that they were a couple. Every Saturday night Susanna picked Joel up. Maybe he should have felt weird about being a teenage boy in the passenger side of a car being driven by a teenage girl. But he didn't. In fact he kind of liked it. The car had those little triangular vent windows. The kind you didn't roll up and down but pushed in and out. Joel liked to fiddle with the one on the passenger side as they drove, feeling the breeze hit him at different angles and at different speeds. Reaching over with his other hand he could touch Susanna's leg, her face, her hair, whenever he wanted. Once and awhile they would go to a movie or a party first, but mostly they'd drive straight to the Korean owned grocery store where all you had to do to buy beer was pat your pockets and say "I must have forgot it" when the owner asked you for I.D. Then they'd drive somewhere and talk. These marathon sessions were a revelation to Joel. He didn't know he had that much talk inside him. It was like each of them was trying to download their entire pasts, presents and futures and do it all at once. They talked like they were on some kind of drug, they talked like they'd been stranded on a desert island for twenty years hopelessly thirsty for human contact, they talked like they'd die if they didn't.

The talking was coiled up in kisses, then touching, and so on down the line, until it all got jumbled up in his mind. Joel was a virgin and knew that on one of these dates he was going to have sex. But he wasn't in a hurry. Like the planes they watched take off and land when they drove out to the barbed wire fence of the Air Force base; it was on the horizon, ETA—TBA. When it did happen it was quick, and sweet, and they didn't stop talking before, after, or even during.

The American Youth Boxing Association season was a round-robin tournament where everybody fought everyone in their weight class twice and then the two with the best records fought each other for the championship. They were held Friday nights—a packed card in an even more packed gym, the Kiwanis Club he and his father had been to just a year ago.

Susanna came to see his first fight, waiting out in hall as he exited the locker room to give him a good luck kiss. His father was there too, slapping him on the back and saying, "Eye of the tiger."

Susanna sat a few rows from ringside. His father took a more analytical perch high up in the rafters. There was such a contrast between the brightness of the ring and the relative darkness of the stands, that both Susanna and his father disappeared once Joel stepped between the ropes to duck under the curtain of light and enter the ring.

He lost the fight in a split-decision. When he'd showered and dressed and came out of the locker room Susanna was there.

"I'm so proud of you," she said. "I don't know anyone who would do what you just did. I mean wow."

Joel shrugged.

"Your father had to go. He said to tell you *You win, you win.*

You lose, you win. But he said it like in the voice of the Godfather or something."

Joel just nodded. Robert De Niro. *Raging Bull.*

But despite the loss in that first fight it turned out Joel was actually pretty good. His father drove him to every fight and Susanna drove him home, always on a "scenic" route that involved either a park or a parking lot. His mother refused to go to his fights. Then she went to one. Then she absolutely refused ever to go again. Like his nickname said, his style was one of careful defense and purposeful jabbing. His wins came when the judges found this style artful. His losses came when the judges, like his opponents, grew frustrated at his refusal to do anything more. But the former outweighed the latter and halfway through the season his record was 6-3.

They were having fondue for dinner, the three of them— Joel, his father, and his mother. They sat around a big pot of hot oil in the middle of the table, its round belly tethered to a socket in the wall by a long electric cord, each one of them equipped with a skinny skewer. They had fondue for dinner, something that to Joel was an embarrassing relic from the seventies, on an unusually regular basis. Joel was convinced that it was his father's favorite meal because it allowed for maximum performance time as Joel and his mother, a submissive and captive audience, waited for each individual bite of meat, each morsel of vegetable, to slowly cook.

But tonight the food sizzled away in silence. Joel held a piece of chicken, about the size and shape of a cashew, in the oil with one hand while with the other he took bites from the ham sandwich he'd made for himself in anticipation of the fondue. His mother anxiously checked and rechecked her crescent of onion to measure its progress. His father wasn't eating at all, just staring into the oil, a liquid windshield onto what no one knew. Finally he spoke.

"The re-lo we've been talking about? It doesn't look like it's going to happen. It's not for lack of trying I promise. But then, hey? We're happy here. Right honey?"

His mother nodded. "Very," she said.

"And Joel you've got that thing you're involved with and a girlfriend too. A pretty girlfriend. Why mess with that?"

Joel nodded and took out the now cooked chicken, blew on it twice, and popped it in his mouth.

One night, not long after the fondue announcement, Joel's father slept out in the garage inside his car. Inside the house Joel and his mother could hear him listening to the radio and assumed he had simply fallen asleep, though why he was listening to the radio in the car in the garage in the first place was a bit of a mystery. But then he slept there again the next night. The next two nights he slept inside, in bed. But the night after that he was back out in the car. It became a semi-regular thing with seemingly no pattern and no point. There was no fight going on between his father and mother. Apparently this was just a hobby of some sort like when his father had for a period built model planes in the den, or when he set-up an easel in the backyard and went out with watercolors, or his origami and cryptology phases. Evidently this hobby was called "car-sleeping."

Joel's bedroom was almost directly above the garage and at night, in bed, he could hear the low murmur of the radio below playing classical music. His father seemed happy enough to Joel. Each morning, when he came through the door that connected the garage with the kitchen, he had a big smile and a thumbs-up as Joel sat at the table eating breakfast and his father headed for the coffee machine. Still, upstairs at night Joel felt like he was listening in on some sort of bizarre suicide. The closed garage. The fluid glow of the dashboard. Only instead of carbon monoxide the air was being filled with the sounds of Tchaikovsky and Beethoven.

As usual he was at the heavy bag. He had gotten strong and now he brought the dead thing to life, each one of his punches causing the bag to move in wide, wobbly arcs. Tomas, a bantam weight a year older than Joel, came over to the bag along with Hector and Marcos who stood a little behind him.

"Yo, Jabber," Tomas said, resting his arm around the bag.

"Yeah," Joel said continuing to punch. Tomas's weight slowed the bag down but the bag continued to move and Tomas swayed a little with it like he was on the deck of a boat out at sea.

"Hector's girlfriend is having a party Monday night," he nodded his head towards Hector and Hector dipped his chin once. "Her parents are gone. You want to come?"

Joel stopped punching and looked at their faces, trying to read if this was an honest invitation or if it was just for sport, that they needed somebody to be the joke of the party. Some sort of high school version of pin-the-tail-on-the-donkey. But he decided it was worth the risk. This was his first chance at fitting in. Besides, he could always leave.

"Sure," he said.

Tomas gave an address. "You know where that is?"

He did. The main part of the city, the urban area, was laid out in a simple grid. It was only when you got out to the sub-urbs where Joel lived that the streets got complicated, with names instead of numbers and more elaborate, winding paths.

"I'll find it," he said.

"Good. See you Monday *mano*."

He didn't bring Susanna. He told her about it but he said it was a boxing thing, a guy thing. She said she understood but Joel wasn't completely sure that he did. He didn't know what to expect at the party and he worried that his not wanting her there showed he was afraid. Was he afraid of what was going to happen to him as a white boy at a Mexican party? Was that racist? If so then what did it say if in the back of his mind he was also worried what would happen to a white girl?

Ironically, the night of the party he felt like a girl himself— he couldn't decide what to wear. Jeans and a t-shirt is what he would have worn to any other party, but he thought somehow that might seem disrespectful. A lot of the Mexican kids at the gym seemed very particular about their clothes, their hair, getting into passionate debates about product and shaving techniques and a lot of other stuff that the guys at Joel's school never talked about. But he didn't want to overdo it either. That would be the most embarrassing. So he went with jeans, but put on a dark button-up shirt made out of some sort of soft but heavy material that his mother had bought for him to wear for his yearbook picture.

He left his house early. He rode his bicycle toward town and stopped at the first bar he saw.

"No way, out," the bartender said as soon as Joel walked inside. "I don't care what you've got in your pocket that says otherwise I'm not serving you."

"No," said Joel. "I need to call a cab."

"Go outside," the bartender said. "I'll call you one."

As he waited Joel stashed his bike behind two dumpsters at the back of the parking lot. He'd never had an occasion to own a lock.

He had the cabbie drop him off a couple blocks short of the address, paid him and then walked to the house. Should he knock? Probably not. So he just opened the door and went inside. He saw instantly how needlessly he had worried about overdoing it. The clothes in his closet didn't even make that a possibility. He owned nothing that came close to what he saw. The guys wore slick, shiny shirts with fancy designs, along with silky slacks and polished leather shoes. And then there were the girls. Their clothes were not something you'd see in the halls of his school. Tight and bright, a combination that managed to be somehow both frivolously child-like and seriously adult.

Even though he felt like there was a spotlight on him, no one seemed to take particular notice as he came in the room. The living room was too filled with bodies for anything as trivial as his arrival to standout. He stood for a few minutes—taking in the scene, thinking briefly about leaving—then he spotted Tomas and made his way over to him.

"Amigo, you're here," Tomas said and reached out a hand.

Joel went to shake it but instead Tomas gave it a sideways slap with the palm of his hand and then another, reverse slap with the back. Then he made his hand into a fist which Joel tapped with his own.

"Let's get you set-up," Tomas said.

The room was heavy with perfume and cologne, so thick that Joel could feel it in the back of his throat. He followed Tomas to the kitchen where the little counter was stacked with beer and wine and all manner of booze. But Tomas directed him over to the kitchen table where a big bowl full of red punch sat next to a stack of red plastic Solo cups. Tomas dipped one of the cups directly into the bowl and handed it to Joel.

"Jungle juice," he said and slapped him on the back. "Make yourself at home."

Everyone was standing, either talking or dancing or both. Joel had no one to talk to and he had never in his life so much as contemplated dancing. So he made his way to an empty sofa and sat down. He sipped at the jungle juice, but nervously, so that even though he took only a little amount each time he raised it to his lips, he did it so many times so quickly that the drink was almost instantly gone.

Joel got up off the sofa and returned to the kitchen. The punch bowl was empty. Instead a group of about five kids were gathered around the table smoking a bowl. One of them wordlessly handed it to him with a lighter. Joel had smoked pot at a few parties. In fact he and Susanna had gotten high together in her parent's basement one night and watched an old movie from their childhoods. Nostalgia mixed with the weed had transformed it into something that seemed very profound at the time but then completely ludicrous the next day.

Joel took the pipe. He clicked the flint wheel of the lighter and put the flame to the bowl. He breathed deep and held it for as long as he could. Then he let the smoke out in one big coughing cloud.

The guy who had given him the pipe laughed.

"If you don't cough, you don't get off," he said.

With watering eyes Joel tried to hand it back to him. But the guy waved his hand indicating the other way. Of course, Joel thought, and embarrassed handed it to the next person in the circle, a girl in a neon yellow halter top to his left.

Joel looked at his watch. He would have sworn he'd been at the party for at least an hour but it had been barely twenty minutes. So he stepped out of the circle, took a warm beer from one of the cases on the counter and went back to the safe anchor of the sofa.

He sat there nursing the beer, this time really concentrating on going slow. For the first time since he'd been there he paid attention to the music that was playing. He'd been so nervous up to now that he hadn't really registered it even though the decibels were rattling the room. The song that was currently playing sounded like it might be familiar but he couldn't tell for sure. It was so loud it could have been almost any song. Its point wasn't to be heard but to be felt. He looked around the room and watched the girls gyrate, the guys cooly snake their bodies in sync with them.

Joel was ready to get up and go for another beer, maybe try to find Tomas again or even Hector or Marcos, but before he could a girl came and sat next to him.

She smiled. He nervously worked the tab on the beer can he was holding back and forth until it broke off. He was waiting for her to say something but apparently she wasn't going to.

"Hi," he said just to get it over with.

"Hi," she said back.

More silence. The girl continued sitting there, smiling, seemingly expecting something from him.

"I'm Joel," he said, holding out his hand.

She laughed, taking his hand by the fingers and turning it in such a way that the handshake became kind of dainty.

"I am Sofia," she said.

"Nice," Joel said. "Pretty."

"Thank you. You are a fighter, no? A boxer?"

"Yeah. I am. How'd you know that?"

"Oh, I can tell. You have the look." She laughed. "Plus my sister told me."

"Who's your sister?"

"Brianna. But you would know her as Hector's girlfriend."

Joel did a quick calculation in his head.

"Your sister is Hector's girlfriend. And this is her house. So this is your house too? This is your party?"

"No. It's my sister's party."

She explained that she was only a freshman. That her sister had told her to clear out for tonight. To go to a movie or something. But none of her friends were allowed out on a Monday night. And surely not to go to a movie. So here she was.

"No friends of your own here," Joel said. "So you came over to talk to the dork on the sofa."

Sofia smiled.

"Something like that."

"I would like to meet your sister. Hector is here? I haven't seen him yet."

"He's not, they are broken up tonight. But just for tonight probably. Or the week at most. That's their thing. Drama."

"Do you drink beer?" Joel asked her holding up the can like an idiot, as if he needed to explain what beer was—him, the sophisticated sophomore.

"I have," she said.

"Would you like one?"

"O.K."

"I'll be right back, don't let any other dorks take my place."

Joel went to the kitchen and grabbed two beers, cold ones this time from the refrigerator, then went back to the sofa and handed Sofia a beer. They both opened their cans, the two shpptz almost in unison.

Sofia took a sip. Joel took a long pull that emptied almost half the can. They hit another silence. Joel looked around at the other girls in the room. He was struck by how much make-up they had on. Much more than any girl wore at his school, although he wondered if maybe it only seemed like more because it looked different on their skin, or maybe it was an effect of the much brighter colors they went for.

Sofia, by contrast, was dressed in a way Joel was much more at ease with. She wore no make-up, or if she did she did in a way that made it seem like she wasn't wearing any. Like him, she had opted for jeans. And she wore a white blouse made out of some very soft gauzy material.

"Do you think I'm pretty?"

Joel was taken aback. Less by the question than by the way she seemed to have read his mind. Ever since she had sat down all he could think about was how pretty she was.

"Well, yeah. Of course," he said.

"You're just saying that. If you thought I was ugly you would still say that."

"No I wouldn't. I mean I wouldn't call you ugly. I wouldn't be mean. But I wouldn't say you were pretty. I'd find some other word. A word that doesn't matter in this situation because you actually are very, very pretty."

"What's pretty about me?"

He wanted to say "your face" but that was so general it meant nothing. And he couldn't say anything about her body although through the softness of the blouse and the tightness of the jeans he could tell it too was very pretty. So finally he just said the most true thing he could find words for even though he knew it sounded like a lie because it was so cliche.

"Your eyes"

"What about my eyes?"

It was a good question. Joel thought about how all eyes are basically the same, if you looked at them in a laboratory or something, so how was it that some almost seemed to speak while others said nothing.

"I don't know," Joel said. "They remind me of coffee."

"Coffee," Sofia said. "I like that."

The conversation threatened to stall again so he just kept on talking.

"But I mean your whole face too. Everything. You are actually beautiful."

"If you really thought so," Sofia said. "You would come up with some clever way to try and get me to show you my room."

"I guess I don't know any clever ways to do that."

"Well you could try just asking."

"May I see your room?"

"Yes, you may."

She led him upstairs to her room, one she obviously shared with her sister. Or a sister. It was small. Just a dresser and two twin beds with a nightstand in-between. On the wall was a poster of Michael Jackson and a bunch of pictures torn from magazines, people he assumed were famous but didn't recognize. Hispanic stars he figured. Or maybe the term was Latino. Sofia went over and sat on one of the beds. He went to sit on the other one but she shook her head and patted the spot next to her.

"Won't your sister come in?"

"No. She will be partying for hours and even if she did come upstairs with somebody she would go to my parents' bedroom. Bigger bed."

He nodded and then leaned forward and kissed her. She kissed him back. They kissed gently for a while and then she touched his shoulder. He touched hers. She trailed her hand down and felt his chest. He did the same, gently cupping a hand over one of her breasts. She wore a lacy bra that rode low on her breasts, making it easy to tug it down slightly, just enough to gently stroke the nipple with a finger. It went on like that, her doing a sort of silent lead by touching him somewhere and him following suit.

But then it stalled out. And then it went in reverse. She brought her hand up to his elbow, then his shoulder again. And then his face. So he took a risk. He put a hand on the upper part of her leg and then, when she didn't object, gently massaged between her thighs with his thumb.

She stopped kissing him and leaned back on the bed, propping herself up with her elbows. She moaned softly. Then, as he began to rub with a little more purpose, she suddenly sat up and draped her arms around his neck.

"That tickles," she said in a soft whisper. Her face was next to his, their cheeks touching, her mouth was right at his ear.

But he wasn't sure what he had heard. Or rather what it meant. Tickle was a good thing right? It's a positive word. But it also isn't. Tickling is fun for the tickler. When you're being tickled the thing you want most in the world is for it to stop.

So Joel stopped. They kissed a little more and then Joel said, "Maybe I should get going."

The "maybe" was supposed to be a huge door for Sophia to walk through. But instead she said, "I like you very much," and then quickly looked at the floor, embarrassed.

"I like you very much too," Joel said. They both sat there for a few minutes but when she didn't say anything more he felt awkward and so he left, Sofia still sitting on the bed, eyes cast down. He went downstairs, found a barely coherent Tomas, said thank you and then left the party.

It was much easier to get a cab in Sophia's neighborhood. Two blocks from her house was a liquor store that let him use their phone. On the bike ride back home he ran through several dozen scenarios in which he might be able to see Sophia again. A few of them were possible, none of them were plausible.

When he got home he was exhausted. He didn't even bother to undress but just fell onto the bed with everything, including his shoes still on. He ran the word "tickle" around and around in his head. *That tickles my fancy. Doctor, my throat has a tickle can you do something about it? It tickled me pink. Tickle-Me-Elmo. I couldn't stand it, it almost tickled me to death.* It was all in how you said it. But how did she say it? In a breath too soft for connotation. She must have wanted him to stop or she wouldn't have said anything. Or maybe it was a moment meant to give him the OK. For him to take charge. To be a man. He thought about how he left. With her looking down at the floor. Not looking at him because she was sorry to have disappointed him? Or looking down because she felt rejected and embarrassed by him?

He woke with an aching erection. Not just a throbbing stiffness in his dick but a soreness that extended to his entire groin. He knew the term for this of course. "Blue balls." He'd heard the phrase many times since all the way back to junior high or probably before. It always made him think of the girl with the gum in the Willy Wonka movie. The cure of course was simple—you jacked-off. He unbuttoned the jeans he'd slept in, lifted the elastic waistband of his underwear up and over the swollen member and looked at it. There was an old idea that got thrown around the gym sometimes. The theory was that if you abstained from sex it made you stronger. No one to his knowledge actually did it. It was used mainly to tease the guys without girlfriends. "Hey, make sure you lay off the sex tonight," they'd say knowing full well that their target had no chance of having sex that night. Or any night soon.

Maybe somewhere in the back of his mind that myth was part of the justification. But it's not why he did what he did. What he was going to do didn't have an easy explanation, even for himself. His dick hurt, his balls hurt even more, but for some reason he wanted that ache, he wanted to keep it, to nurse it even.

It stayed with him through the week, the ache in his genitals. The erection itself waxed and waned a bit. It was worst in the shower and under the sheets at night. At school he wore the tails of his shirt untucked, sometimes adding the double protection of shielding it with a text book. He had a wet dream one night and worried that that would ruin it but it was still there the next day, his dick as heavy and dense as ever, like a roll of coins that never left his pocket.

He avoided Susanna. She'd called the day after the party asking him how it was. He said OK. She asked if he wanted to go get something to eat. He said no. Homework. They saw each other at school but he kept the conversations short, making up some other place he had to be, some other thing he needed to do. Telling her maybe he had the flu or something.

He missed her though. Terribly. Who was that guy they read in English class that said something about love only being measured by how much you missed the person when they weren't there. Shakespeare? Probably. Wasn't everything Shakespeare?

On Thursday he went down to the high school's gym. It was out of season so the volleyball team only practiced twice a week. They'd finished third in the state tournament that year. Joel could only go to the home games, because he couldn't drive to away games and Susana was required to go on the team bus. But he watched her home games as faithfully as she watched his fights. She was good, as far as Joel could tell, and the coach used her for a variety of purposes. She was often the libero, what they called a sort of roaming defensive specialist, she could dig with the best of them but had a mean jump serve too.

The metal doors to the gym, as heavy and thick as a bank vault, were propped open. Like a thief he stood half hidden by them and watched the practice. The wooden court was polished until it glistened like an ice rink; their mascot in the middle, baring its teeth. Susanna and the rest of the team were wearing the black uniform pants they always did—shockingly tight and impossibly short. As Joel watched he found he kept thinking about the moon. Was it simply the ball, a white so bright that it looked freshly bleached? Or was it the way the ball floated in the air as if at zero gravity? Or was it maybe the girls themselves?

He didn't think he did anything different. When he got into the ring he went into his same mode of solid defense and careful offense. But in the third round it happened. He hadn't planned it exactly, but at one point his opponent went to back up, to regroup, and in doing so dropped a glove down to his side. But he did it carelessly, dropping the glove first before starting his retreat. So Joel dropped a glove too. Not in order to rest and reset, but so that he could rotate further and then uncoil his right fist into his opponent's face.

He caught him on the side of the head and the next thing Joel knew his opponent was sitting down on the mat, looking at him with an angry scowl on his face but unable to get up. The referee rushed over and began checking his vitals almost simultaneously as he began the count. It was a quick count. They were teenagers and no one was taking any chances with a teenager's head. The referee got to ten, motioning with both hands that the fight was over as a doctor rushed into the ring. Joel had his first knockout.

There was no fanfare. The crowd didn't pour out of the stands and hoist him onto their shoulders. In fact, the next two fighters were in their corners and being announced before Joel had even gotten out of the ring.

He went to the locker room and as soon as he could get Juan Carlos to cut the tape on his hands and wrists he went into a bathroom stall and masturbated. Then he showered and dressed. Susanna and his Dad were waiting outside the locker room to congratulate him—Susanna hugging him, his father saying "nice win."

Afterwards, parked in the car with Susanna he came before she'd even unzipped his pants. She laughed. "You missed me!" she said and kissed him on the cheek. But later, when he entered her, something was different. He was still rock hard but having come twice already he had a control he hadn't had before. They fucked for a long time and the longer they did the more the rhythm changed, the more Susanna changed. Her face went from the faintly soft smile it usually had during sex to what Joel thought might be a slight grimace. The noises she made changed too, from something like "oh" to something that sounded very close to "ow."

"Wow," she said when they finished. But neither of them said a word on the way home.

The summer brought two changes. The first was a new

house. Joel and his mother weren't even informed until the night his father had the papers in front of him at the kitchen table. It was a house even further in the suburbs. It had twice as much square footage as they needed, twice as many bedrooms, twice as many bathrooms. There was a pool in the back and a yard big enough that it required a crew of three Mexicans to come out every other week to maintain it.

The second thing was his sixteenth birthday. There was a car in the driveway awaiting him after he'd passed his driver's test. A two-year old used Toyota Camry. Red.

He'd finished the boxing season with 11 wins and 7 losses. Fourth place in his division. It was a fantastic first go Juan Carlos said to him. Next year will be better. But even as he nodded at Juan Carlos and thanked him, Joel knew there would be no next year. The car allowed him, when school was over for the summer, to replace the gym with a part-time job at an amusement park warehouse where he traded the heavy bag for lifting large boxes of frozen chicken strips and ice cream sandwiches from delivery pallets to giant walk-in freezers.

He also used the car to go visit his father.

His father was still living in their old house which had yet to sell. Why his father was staying there was unspoken at least to Joel. But once a week or so he'd drive over. Most of their possessions had made the move to the new house even if his father hadn't. There was a mattress on the living room floor next to a beat-up armchair. A pile of clothes, dirty or clean Joel couldn't tell, was in one corner. Joel sat in the armchair while his father crouched on the mattress.

It was on one of these visits that out of nowhere his father said, "You know that poster you used to have?" He jerked his head upwards towards the second floor above them. "The one over your bed?"

"Sure," said Joel.

"I listened to that fight," said his father. "On the radio. 1965. I was in my second or third year of graduate school. Studying for some exam or another. But I had the fight on. The fight was a big deal. Huge. I mean it was the sixties. The *Sixties,* you know? Malcolm X had just been assassinated for god's sake. And Kennedy of course. King not yet but coming. And here were not just two black guys but a black guy and a black *muslim.*"

His father paused and Joel could almost see the newsreel running through his father's head.

"All this anticipation but it turned out the fight was over like that," his father snapped his fingers. "You barely had enough time to register that the fight had even started." He shook his head. "You know what they called that punch? The one that got Liston?"

Joel shook his head.

"The Phantom Punch. There were people at the fight, eyewitnesses, who swore up and down, still do, that Ali never landed it. That Liston had gone down on his own."

"Why would he do that?"

"Who knows? The main theory was that the mob had fixed the fight and it had just been a bad job of acting. Bad on Liston's part. Ali wasn't capable of doing anything bad in front of a camera."

"Is that what you think? That it was fixed?"

"I don't know. Like I said, I was listening to in on the radio. No Phantom Punch is going to make it through a dime store transistor. And damn that Ali was fast. Strong too. But his speed was something else. I'd see Ali fight over the years on TV and sometimes you couldn't believe the two people in the ring were from the same planet. It was like Ali had dropped down from outer space. But could he be that fast? Invisible fast? Phantom Punch fast? A knockout punch is a pretty hard thing to miss."

Even with the unconventional living arrangement, it was a nice summer. When Joel wasn't at work at the warehouse, and Susanna wasn't at work at a coffee shop downtown, she would come over to the house and the two of them would lounge poolside, moving between the pool and the desert heat of the patio to the TV inside the house and the glacial air-conditioning of the "den." Occasionally his mother would even bring them sun tea or those double-barreled popsicles that he hadn't had since he was a kid.

With 2,200 square feet and only his mom around, it was easy for Joel and Susanna to discreetly slip upstairs to his room. The sex he and Susanna had grown into was good. More like adults, he figured, more conscious of the other's pleasure. It often felt like they were taking turns with their individual pleasures rather than the mad, messy rush it had been when they were first dating. But that night in the car after the knockout nagged at him. Why was it better to go a long time? It felt good, sure, but he remembered how when they first started having sex he'd come inside Susanna within minutes, seconds maybe. She was so beautiful. A few minutes was actually an accomplishment. He felt he could have come just looking at her. So what did it mean that he could last longer now? Isn't that why people said that male porn stars were actually gay? That they had "stamina" because they didn't really like women? And on the subject of porn stars—why were bigger dicks better dicks? That night with Susanna he felt he may have actually been hurting her. That was good?

His father, wordlessly, moved into the new house in September even though the old one still had not sold. By then Susanna was off to college and Joel's relationship with her took the predictable slow fade. Joel knew it was inevitable so it surprised him how painful it actually ended up being.

In late October Joel came home from school. He threw his backpack down on the kitchen table and called out "Mom?" There was no answer. What he did hear was the sound of something in the garage.

His father was sitting in the driver's seat. Loud music, probably by some unhinged German, was playing on the radio. It was way too early for his father to be home from work, but then again the back of his head was missing. Joel got in on the other side of the car and sat down next to him. The gunshot through the mouth had left his face remarkably intact. Just some stuff fanning up his cheeks, powder burn Joel guessed, from a distance it might have been mistaken for five o'clock shadow. The rest of the stuff—the blood, the bone, the brain, whatever else his father carried around inside there—covered the entire backseat and most of the back windshield. Joel sat for a while in the passenger seat. He would have sat longer but he didn't know when his mother would be home. So after a few minutes, five or maybe ten, he turned off the radio and went inside to call an ambulance.

It was a couple of years later, when Joel was packing for college that he came across the old Ali poster rolled up in his closet. He'd already bought a poster for his new dorm room, one from a Godard movie that he hoped would make him seem cool. Or at least smart. He took the Ali poster and laid it on his bedroom floor, using a dictionary on one end and a thesaurus on the other to keep it flat. He looked at Ali. He looked at Liston. He thought about the slippery authority of what we can see, and the power and speed of what we can't.

CORRIDOR

(Camouflage Don DeLillo, *Mao II*, Chapter 7)

You are walking down a long corridor lined with paper. Squared slices of moonlight tacked up like fish scales. Adhesive sheets words cling to. There is a feeling of intense solitude in the corridor, intense even for you. You feel the loneliness on your tongue. It tastes like tin.

Perhaps if you were to make it out of the corridor, limousines would pull up, eager to escort the feeling to a set of far away coordinates. 8th and Broadway. 11 West and 53rd. Any X. Any Y.

But you stick to the corridor. Make yourself at home. Take off your tweed jacket, bend down and loosen the laces of your shoes. Nothing will come of any of this. But you enjoy how the paper ripples with even the tiniest movement.

BOOKS

(Camouflage Don DeLillo, *Mao II*, Chapter 1)

I shoplifted my first book. It was a collection of poems by a poet who lived in our city. I think I was trying satisfy myself such things were made by people, with shape and earth-rooted mass. It worked only marginally.

Getting a new book was like picking at an infection from a beautiful disease. "Could be worse," my father said. He'd shrug and give me a five or maybe a ten, whatever thin bill was in his wallet. When you walked into a bookstore the slick spines on the shelves gave off a charged heat. The webbed secret between writer and reader.

If you were proverbially abducted by proverbial aliens how would you describe a book to them? Could you get across how in books words become living shadows that speak? Or that the lines are like blacktop streets lit by the moon? Maybe it would be easier just to say books are waking dreams.

If you did somehow make all that clear--how would you explain their extinction? Replaced by shiny new electric-chair canvases. Not touched but pulled from the air. A synthetic mass language. Books too flexible and accommodating to fight back. Caught up in the forever of a planetary work-in-progress.

ROTE

(Camouflage David Foster Wallace, *Infinite Jest*)

It's not all German plays, smeary sets, Lemon Pledge
dick-sucking, street corners of broken soft light where men sit
shirtless and deep-socketed, not even a sign or a hat for
pocket-change,* orange caps of Gatorade strewn about like
pogs, the empty bottles filled with piss in lieu of a loo; it is also
bare-feet, Oreo cookies and psychic flow, totally pleased and
amused, inside the TV is a boundless jewelry box, the friend-
ly lobotomizing microwave on the floor for convenience, the
crappy stereo thirty years old that can still turn the living room
into an amphitheater, spreading out sounds so overly familiar
they're hymns, no sadness here—it splatters into a massive,
glowing euphoria.

*Just hoping if they stare long enough quarters and dimes will up and
grow out of the sidewalk.

ALBUM TITLES

(Camouflage Don DeLillo, *Mao II*, Chapter 14)

    --Imagine Explanation
    --Normal Standards of Behavior
    --Extraordinarily Slight
    --Conversation Stretched Flat
    --Eternal Insidedness
    --Puzzled Possibility
    --Imagine Fact Not Finished
    --Second Chances (Collecting Undyingly)
    --Honestly Thought Miss You
    --Wettish Pages
    --Visual Litter
    --Extraordinarily Erased

PHOTOGRAPHS

(Camouflage Don DeLillo, *Mao II*, "In Beirut")

Photographs are relentless light. They reciprocate the silence of things, the quiet we are usually too noisy to hear. We are allowed to stand within the image out-of-body. How did human memory work before photographs? Because now our forgotten lives are escorted back to us in these tissues of light. Pictures large enough to be driven into the human skull. Massive and intense enough to make the invention of stories necessary.

ALONE

(Camouflage Don DeLillo, *Mao II*, Chapters 8 and 9)

My father would sometimes pull away from us. He would depart the room and seek out a place where he could be by himself. He left us and carved out an empty space. If he knew why he needed this kind of desertion he never spoke it. I imagine it as a subtle inward twist because I've felt it myself. The way remoteness gives a familiar intimacy to a place. If our home was a sentence my father, in his seclusion, was a comma. He sought out aloneness like he was looking for a place to smoke a cigarette. The calm light of the abandoned afternoon, no doubt, a kind of nicotine.

GALAXY

As word of my wife's death spread throughout the neighborhood, baking dishes wrapped in tinfoil and stacks of brightly colored Tupperware started showing up on the doorstep. They were sorely needed. It was always a happy sight when I pulled into the driveway after picking Henley up from school, or returning from the gym, and saw something warm and self-contained waiting by the front door.

My wife Ashley and I had an arrangement where she did most of the cooking and I did most of the cleaning. Now I found myself standing in the kitchen wearing a "Kiss the Cook" apron and holding a spatula, totally lost at sea. Mostly I just did whatever Henley told me to do. A grilled cheese sandwich was her go-to breakfast. When I expressed reservations about the nutritional value she said, "What's the bread on a grilled cheese sandwich?" I didn't answer so she answered for me. "*Toast,*" she said in complete disbelief at my stupidity. "In every country except the U.S.," she continued, "Cheese is a common, even essential, breakfast component." I wondered if that was true and if so how she knew. "What about the potato chips?" I said. "Dad, tell me, is there any real difference between a potato chip and a hash brown?"

So the doorstep dinners were a welcomed surprise.

This was wholesome home-cooked food. Some even consisted of multiple courses. It was food I could feel good about giving to a growing eight-year old. Each dish came with a note expressing condolences and explaining what the dish was, with helpful instructions about how to reheat and/or assemble it. Some of the women also left their phone numbers. If they were lucky enough to have a lowercase "i" or "j" in their name these women, the phone number ones, substituted a little heart for the dot above the letter. The others, the i-and-j-less, just drew a big heart that lassoed their entire name.

While I was happy to be feeding Henley real food, I was in training. My diet consisted of smoothies and numerous powders. The most I could do with the grief meals was to eat whatever protein there was and pick a few veggies out of a pasta primavera.

There was a fight coming up over in Galaxy. I'd seen the flier in the grocery store, up front with the aquariums of gum balls and jaw-breakers. I pulled it off its thumbtack and when I got home stuck it to our refrigerator with a pineapple shaped magnet. After a couple of days looking at it I went upstairs to the drawer where I kept my workout stuff and got out the three-ring binder. It was filled with sheets of paper in plastic sleeves. The sleeves told me when to run, when to lift, when to spar, when to go to the dojo.

I could do almost everything dictated by the three-ring binder while Henley was at school. The one exception was my morning run. I was in a spot, but I couldn't neglect cardio. People were always underestimating and therefore neglecting cardio. That first morning was tough. I must have checked the deadbolt a dozen times. But finally I started on my way through the early dawn of our neighborhood. The air was a blue you could almost touch and as the minutes progressed the sidewalks slowly turned the color of early season watermelon. But all I could think of was Henley alone in the house. The first couple of miles were OK. But in the middle miles my anxiety began to build and along with it my pace. The final mile or so was a dead sprint home as all manner of horrific images raced through my mind. But Henley was fine, snoozing away in her bed as I stood panting and gulping over her. It was pretty much the best cardio I'd ever had.

With my three-ring binder I was lucky. I had something. Henley, though, had nothing but school. We'd always stressed school, my wife and I, and Henley's report cards were seldom less than perfect. Still, I couldn't help but think that school—with its word-searches and flashcards, the rote sing-songs of presidents and state capitols—probably wasn't the ideal environment for mourning the death of your mother.

At home she seemed all right, considering. Except her hygiene. Her hygiene was definitely suffering. Forget brushing her teeth, or oh my god flossing, it was all I could do when she got smelling too ripe to beg, plead, and cajole until she agreed to take a shower. She locked the bathroom door, but I could hear the shower going. Still, I wouldn't put it past her to just sit on the toilet seat with a book while she let the water run.

But I couldn't be too hard on her. I was letting my household duties fall into neglect too. Henley liked to take a finger and write her name in the dust that had collected everywhere. There were almost as many dirty dishes and used glasses sitting on the bookshelves as there were books. Henley's Doritos and Fritos bags showed up in curious places. The toilets were getting that funky water-level ring of algae. The kitchen counter felt like a movie theater floor.

As much as I would have liked to, I couldn't workout 24/7. There were gaps—holes that had to try and be filled in some way. The hours between my final nine o'clock protein drink and my five o'clock morning run were the worst. I broke the "no alcohol" part of the three-ring binder many times contending with those hours, trying to sweet talk sleep.

Late one night, with sleep clearly not coming, I crept into Henley's room and scooped all the clothes I could into a laundry basket. Both our bedrooms had floors practically knee-deep in dirty clothes. While the machine did its shake and spin in the basement, I sat in the living room sipping bourbon and watching a cop show on TV through one of Henley's ornate dust signatures running across the screen.

When the washer buzzer went off I went down and moved the damp ball of clothes to the dryer. I cranked the dial to sixty minutes, the furthest it would go. The dryer was an ancient thing, maybe as old as the house itself, and it put out an unreal amount of heat. Sixty minutes was too long by at least half an hour. But time was the enemy, or at least not on my side. I sat down on the basement floor with my back against a wall and a fresh drink in hand. While I listened to the dryer's loud lullaby hum, I started thinking about those little notes on the casseroles and the women who wrote them.

The next night I went to the fold-down desk where I mostly kept bills and took out the notes. I was nowhere near ready to date. I figured I probably never would be. But I pictured a woman's hands gently applying nail polish to Henley's toes as the two talked about feelings. I saw those same hands running a brush through Henley's hair while they laughed about girl stuff I couldn't possibly understand. I saw them hand-in-hand with Henley as they walked through the mall, stepping into stores where Henley could dress up in all sorts of beautiful outfits. A woman friend would be Henley's three-ring binder.

I shuffled through the notes trying to put together names, faces and places. Had I met them at Henley's school? Had we maybe chatted a few times while they were out with their dog and I was walking the mower across the lawn? Or were they Ashley's co-workers? Women who came over for snacks and margaritas some Fridays but whose names, even in the moment, blended together. Sometimes somebody would come pick Ashley up to go to a farmer's market or Sunday matinée, but those were just a honk and an arm out a window waving goodbye.

I decided to call Veronica. She might, I thought, be the woman who I saw riding her bicycle to and from work every day. She wore tight-fitting clothes made from fabrics that looked like they belonged on superheroes.

Veronica sounded relieved when she answered the phone. My name didn't show on her cell which meant I was either a salesman, an emergency, or a creep. I sort of felt like she had me dead-to-rights on all three, but I moved forward and thanked her for the dish she'd brought over (though I had no idea which one) it was so thoughtful, I said, and tasted so good. Turns out she wasn't the bike lady but a woman at Ashley's office. She asked me how I was doing and I said to be honest not real well. We talked a little more and when the call had ended she was coming over on Saturday.

Despite my protests she brought the fixings for dinner. After I helped her move the grocery bags from her car into the kitchen we had a drink. I'd stocked up on wines, both red and white, but she'd brought her own—a rosé. I poured her a glass of the cotton candy colored wine and poured a bourbon for myself, one ice cube.

During my pre-dinner conversation with Veronica, Henley laid on her stomach in front of the TV shouting intentionally wrong answers at Jeopardy and Wheel of Fortune. Actually it was the same wrong answer every time. "What is Kalamazoo?" she screamed.

Veronica and I talked over the din as best we could. It was pretty OK conversation considering she wanted to ask about me and all I wanted to do was tell her about Henley. Veronica was blond, two years younger than me, had no children, was divorced, and owned two car lots in town. I recognized the names because when I drove by them I was always struck by the unconventional uses they found for balloons and streamers.

This was all well and good, but what I was really excited about were the fingers holding Veronica's wineglass. Each very long nail had a tiny nail-polish sunflower on it.

"Did you have those done? At a spa or something?" I asked pointing to her hand. She set the wineglass on the coffee table, spread out her fingers, and held them at arm's length.

"Oh, my. No," she said.

"You did them yourself?"

"Yes."

"Wow."

"It's nothing," she said and picked up her wine.

This one's a keeper I thought.

We had a pleasant dinner except that Veronica eventually brought up the question I'd been dreading—What did I do for a living?

Until recently I could have said "bank teller." Which wasn't exactly a winning answer. But after Ashley, I'd taken all the grief and sick leave I could, and when the checks stopped coming I assumed I'd been let go. But I couldn't say "unemployed." That would be bad. So I told her the truth, although it was more a hobby than a job.

"I do mixed martial arts," I said.

"You mean like fighting?"

I nodded.

"Oh my god! I've seen that on TV, right? I can't watch. Do you get hurt?"

And so the rest of dinner was wasted on a lengthy explanation of the ins and outs of MMA, time that could have been spent focused on Henley who was playing a game where she slid down her chair inch-by-inch until her nose barely peeked out over the table and I told her to sit up.

Still, it seemed like things had gone well. Henley even went to bed without a fuss. But when I came back downstairs after tucking Henley in, Veronica was gone. I stood in the middle of the living room slightly dazed, rewinding back though the events of the evening trying to find something I had done wrong. I actually thought of going out the front door and running after her even though she had a good thirty-minute head start and was in a car. Then I heard a noise. It came from the kitchen.

When I walked in Veronica was at the sink up to her elbows in soap suds.

"Just tidying up a little," she said.

Besides the pile of dishes on the drainage board, and many others air-drying on tea towels, the dishwasher was also whining away. I ran a finger along the countertop. Smooth as an ice rink. She wasn't doing tonight's dishes. She was doing everything.

The next weekend the three of us ordered pizza and watched movies. I discovered that rosé, which I'd bought a case of, went pretty damn well with the pepperoni I picked off a couple slices. This time when I was upstairs putting Henley to bed I heard the cough and purr of the vacuum cleaner. When I came down not only was the carpet clean but the living room had been dusted.

"You've got to stop doing this," I said half-heartedly.

When it came to the physical, Veronica was not shy. But so far I'd managed to juke and feather-step my way around her advances. However, she suddenly stood up on her tip-toes and gave me a peck on the cheek that was too quick for me to duck.

The next weekend we spent a Sunday afternoon out at the lake on Veronica's brother's boat. Henley had a great time but I got the impression the excursion was mostly calculated for me to see Veronica in a bikini. Like I couldn't already tell what was going on under her clothes.

After the day on the boat, Veronica started talking about going out somewhere. A real date. Just the two of us. I said I couldn't leave Henley. "We'll get a babysitter," Veronica said. I shook my head no. What I didn't say, but realized suddenly, was I wasn't worried how Henley would do without me, but that I didn't want to be without Henley.

So Veronica picked us both up in an Audi with mileage that

hadn't yet reached triple digits. She took us to a very posh place, five courses and the revelation of tiramisu for Henley. The one thing Veronica could never seem to understand, no matter how often I explained, was that when I was in training I had to eat certain things and avoid others. That concept just wasn't in her world. I did what I could with the expensive food, did more than I should have, the fight was only a couple of weeks away.

At the house I potato-sacked Henley upstairs, and as I got her settled in bed I had to admit I was more than a little excited about the prospects of what awaited downstairs. Last week Veronica had done the bathroom. The house was now basically spotless. What new twist would she come up with? My bet was on the oven—long yellow gloves, toxic fumes. I was sniffing so often for confirmation that Henley asked me if I was sick. Then she said, "Dad?"

"Yeah?"

"Is Veronica like your girlfriend?"

Damn it. It was supposed to be Veronica and Henley drawing closer, but so far the focus had been on Veronica and me.

"I wouldn't be mad," Henley said during my pause. "She's nice and everything I guess."

"Yes, she is," I said. "But no, she's not my girlfriend."

When I got downstairs the mood was not one of cleaning. The lights in the kitchen were off and there was only one on in the living room. Veronica was sitting under it on the sofa, legs crossed, shadows doing amazing things to her body. She held two large martini glasses in each hand.

"Nightcap?" she said.

I took one of the drinks but sat down in the armchair across from her. I watched her teethe and tongue an olive off a toothpick. My drink was gone in two gulps. Veronica came over to the armchair and sat in my lap. She draped an arm around my neck, turned her head, and gave me a deep kiss.

Ashley had been gone for a little less than three months. When she died I assumed, I hoped, that the last kiss she gave me would be the last one to ever touch my lips. But now there was this. I was trying to think of some way to get Henley back downstairs as a defense, but Veronica grabbed my shoulders and, in a move I wished I had been paying attention to because I could have used it in two weeks, smoothly took us down to the floor with me on top. We kissed again but when she grabbed my ass I did a barrel roll as far away from her as decorum would allow.

I laid there on the floor on my back, not looking at Veronica. "I'm not in love with you."

Veronica crawled over and rested her chin atop the two hands she'd placed on my chest like she was going to perform a gentle method of CPR.

"What do you mean?"

"You're a wonderful person. As a person I care about you a lot. But I'm not in love with you. You know. Romantically? No romantically is the wrong word. I mean big picture. That's what I don't have. A big picture of us."

"Why?" she said.

"I'm not ready, I guess."

"There's no rush."

"I don't think time is the answer," I said.

She was quiet. Hurt obviously. So I flailed around for something to stop that hurt.

"But we can see each other. You could still come over and cook, or maybe we can do laundry together. You know? Separate the whites? Fold when the clothes come out of the dryer. Plus you could start spending more quality time with Henley. I know she'd really like that."

Veronica seemed angry for a moment and then laughed.

"So this whole time I've been going home every night and standing in front of the mirror wondering what was wrong with me."

"I'm sorry. I didn't know I was making you feel rejected. You are extremely attractive. We could I guess maybe later on down the road try to add sex at some point. I can't promise anything, but we could try if it would make you feel better."

"Oh gee, thanks. So you want me to cook and clean and have sex with you? Take care of your little girl? Here's a news-flash. That's a relationship. Hell, that's basically a marriage."

"You're not understanding," I said and searched the ceiling for words.

But Veronica had already gotten up and grabbed her purse. From my spot on the floor I listened to the door slam.

The next night was supposed to have been a "traditional Sunday dinner" as presented by Veronica. I set the table, even using cloth napkins. I opened a chilled bottle of rosé. I thought maybe in the light of day things would be different. But no dice. At six-thirty I got Henley and the two of us drove to KFC where I broke training big time.

The day I left for Galaxy there was a special assembly at Henley's school. At three-thirty parents arrived for an exhi-bition celebrating the Bingerton Mine. It was a yearly exercise in agitprop. Bingerton, an open-pit mine, was the third largest producer of iron in the world and a huge part of the area's econ-omy. It was also likely the source of the extinction of at least one species of bird and an elevated amount of several chemicals in our water system that made bottled water and tap filters must-haves for most people. To combat this image, the mine made many goodwill gestures to the community including a contest every year at the local schools. The winner at each school re-ceived part of an admittedly generous scholarship fund.

This year's topic was "My Mine, Your Mine." The 5th and 6th graders wrote essays. The other grades drew pictures that were on display down the entire length of the school's main hall-way; each one a flattering rendition of the Bingerton Mine. In theory. Half the kids veered wildly off topic the second crayon hit construction paper. There were a dozen or so scenes of the mine under alien invasion. There were also a lot of attempts at ponies which ended-up looking like four-legged worms. I was kind of partial to the kid who drew an army of ninjas skateboarding down the side of the mine. Each picture received a large silver ribbon that said "Fantastic!" in the middle of its flower-like top. They were participation ribbons. The prize pictures received ribbons that were yellow, red, and of course, blue.

I asked Henley to show me hers. It had a silver ribbon attached to it. It didn't have much to do with "My Mine, Your Mine." But if art is supposed to move you then it was definitely art.

I gave Henley's shoulder a squeeze and a kiss on the top of her head.

"I love it, honey," I said. "It's blue ribbon in my book."

The picture that won the actual blue ribbon in Henley's grade showed The Statue of Liberty, a *smiling* Statue of Liberty, perched on the mine with the words "Made in America" fanned across the top in red and blue stars. It was tacky, pandering, and had little imagination. It was no surprise it won First Place.

"I hate it," Henley said. "It's Margaret Van Wagoner's. When they announced the winners yesterday I pointed out to Mrs. Frankel that The Statue of Liberty is made out of copper, not iron. That's why it's green. Oxidation. Plus, it wasn't made in America. It was given to us by France."

"Wow," I said, impressed. "What did Mrs. Frankel say?"

"She said one of the reasons we have contests is not just to learn how to be good winners, but also how to be good losers."

After about twenty minutes we were told to gather in the auditorium. A bunch of kids and several parents rushed to the refreshment table to grab a last minute snickerdoodle. When we were all seated the principal said a few words of introduction and we listened to the two first place essays from the fifth and sixth grades. The principal commented on the prize drawings and then everyone was dismissed. On their way out each kid took their picture and ribbon off the wall. Everyone but Henley.

"I don't want it," she said when I told her to go get it.

"Of course you do."

Henley walked off. I went and got the picture. She was waiting outside next to the truck. I handed it to her and told her to get in.

She was staying with Ashley's brother, Gerald, while I went over to Galaxy for the fight. Technically, he was Ashley's half-brother—fifteen years older from her father's first marriage. When their father died a couple of years ago, since Gerald had never really moved out of the house for any extended period of time anyway, he just sort of stayed there and by squatter's rules or something the house became his.

But Gerald was basically an OK guy. When we got to his place I got out and grabbed Henley's bag from the back of the truck. Gerald had several different video game systems so I expected her to make a beeline for the living room. But instead she was sitting in the passenger side seat, not moving a muscle, her seatbelt still strapped across her chest. I walked over and opened the door.

"What's up?" I said.

In response her head flopped from side to side and her eyes rolled around in their sockets. For good measure she stuck her tongue out of one side of her mouth.

I got it. We were playing "dead."

"Not this, Henley," I said. "Please don't do this."

I unbuckled her seatbelt and pulled her out of the truck but she rag-dolled her limbs and fell to the ground where she lay with her eyes closed and body motionless.

My breath started to catch a little and my heart rate went into double time.

"Get the fuck up now!" I said.

I grabbed her arm hard and yanked her equally hard to her feet.

Tears instantly sprang to her eyes. I didn't even realize I was still gripping her arm. She twisted out of my grasp with two good yanks and ran into the house.

I stood in the driveway shocked. Even Gerald who was walking across the lawn to meet us paused and looked at me in surprise.

I went into the house. I knew I had hurt her. Physically hurt her as well as damaging who knew what all else. Henley was in the living room sort of scrunched up on the far end of the couch. She was crying but when she saw me she stopped, wiped her cheeks with the palms of her hands, and looked away.

"I'm sorry," I said. "I didn't mean to do that. It was wrong. It will never ever happen again. I promise."

Henley just sat there looking sort of like an armadillo with her arms folded tight across her body. It was a move of both protection and defiance.

"Let me take a look at your arm," I said. I was afraid I could have left a welt. But she twisted around and leaned away from me. I gave her a kiss on the cheek which she wiped off with her entire sleeve in one melodramatic sweep. It didn't look like I'd be getting a kiss in return.

Galaxy was a good eight hours away. I got over four hours under my belt before I stopped at a motel for the night. This way I could, hopefully, get somewhere close to eight hours, or at least five, of sleep. When I woke up I would be able to finish the drive and easily make the twelve o'clock sign-in. It was single elimination. You paid $200 and if you made it all the way through your weight class you got $2,000 and a trophy.

I woke up just before five o'clock. My body thought it was going to be let out on its morning run. But training was over. I stepped out of my boxers and got in the shower. After quickly wetting myself down I turned off the water. Standing in the shower, dripping and shivering, I picked up the special coffee mug I'd packed and twirled a fat shaving brush around the inside. I then proceeded to cover my entire body, except my back since Ashley wasn't there, in a thick lather— from my face and neck down to my ankles. I looked and felt like some sort of mutant albino swamp thing. I shaved my body before every tournament. It was my secret weapon, or at least my magic feather. When I finished lathering, I set the mug and brush down on the edge of the tub and clicked open a straight razor. The foam came off in long, smooth strokes like icing on a cake. I rinsed off and emerged from the shower, slick and shiny, a mint condition action figure fresh from the box.

It was Ashley who had come up with it. The idea was that like wind and a cyclist, water and a swimmer, my opponent's blows would slide right off me.

Wind? Water? Try tornado. Tsunami. From the moment I stepped into the cage I got my ass handed to me. Apparently I made it to the second round of the fight. I didn't remember there being a break between rounds, but apparently there was. I didn't remember much except arms and legs, fists and feet, and the upside down face of the referee which made his eyebrows look like two bushy mustaches under each eye. Mercifully, in that second round, my opponent decided to stop wasting energy toying with me and got me in a chokehold. It was the only time that instead of tapping out I flirted with the idea of unconsciousness. It presented itself as an attractive option. I imagined green fields. A breeze. A sleep so deep it turned your bones to Jell-O. But just as I felt my eyelids flutter and my eyeballs start to reach for the back of my head, the referee with the two mustaches stopped the fight.

The next morning I woke up on a blood-soaked pillow. I put it in my roller. I figured if I stole it they might not notice it was gone and even if they did it would be better than leaving the pillow in the room and having it look like there had been a beheading or something.

I went to the lobby in search of food. I was much too late for the hotel's courtesy breakfast hours, but apparently so were a lot of the other guests most of whom had obviously competed in the fights last night because there were some very large people jammed into a very small breakfast alcove. Management, it seemed, didn't feel like telling some 6'6" 230 pound jujitsu expert he couldn't have his waffles and orange juice. It was a little like that scene in Gone With the Wind, the famous one, where the camera pans to a wide shot of all the wounded. The tiny tables in the breakfast alcove sported all manner of cuts, bruises, braces and casts. Men and women both. In fact I saw one couple with symmetrical black eyes—his right, her left. My head was killing me and my ribs hurt every time I swallowed a forkful of scrambled eggs, but despite how badly I'd gotten beat-up my only really bad visible injury was a swollen nose that was busy changing all sorts of interesting colors. I sported two tusks of Kleenex I'd crammed in my nostrils in an effort to stop the bleeding.

I was past checkout time too, but the clerk wasn't budging. Fifty dollars late charge. I asked him if I paid it could I stay in the room a little longer? Just until the maid came and then I'd leave I promised. No, was his curt response. I had to do something about my head. The throbbing was doing weird things to my vision. I couldn't drive. So I asked him where the nearest liquor store was. He pointed across the street.

I bought a tall boy and used the first pull to wash down a handful of aspirin and a couple of Oxies I'd brought in my dopp kit. I laid down in the truck, my knees sticking-up in the cab like it was a shallow bathtub. I used a wadded-up t-shirt for a pillow and when the beer was about half empty I set it on the floorboard, closed my eyes, and went to sleep.

When I woke-up it was late afternoon. Every time I fell asleep I half hoped, half feared I would dream about Ashley. There in the truck cab I didn't dream about Ashley. I dreamt about Veronica. It was a sex dream and it wasn't the first time it had happened. It made me feel like shit of course. But I wondered if maybe all dreams aren't a betrayal of one kind or another.

Henley had unsurprisingly left her drawing in the truck. I sat up and took it off the dash. It was our town, the giant mine looming over it as it did in real life. The picture showed shopping, rollerskating, cooking, walking dogs, biking, swimming almost every activity you could imagine. It was sort of like a game, you could look a long time and then suddenly see something you hadn't seen before. There were probably several dozen people in all. Every one of them was Ashley.

Thanks to my little nap I didn't get back to the city until after eleven that night. But even though I was running late, I stopped at the grocery store. I needed a peace offering. In the frosty abundance of the ice cream freezer I got a gallon of vanilla. On my way to the register I grabbed a two-liter of root-beer. I threw the grocery bag in the back of the truck where I hoped the cool night air would help the ice cream stay frozen.

At Gerald's I knocked softly on the door. He winced when he saw my face.

"Not a good one I guess," he said.

I shrugged.

Gerald pointed to Henley who was curled up in an armchair sound asleep despite the blaring TV. I picked her up and Gerald handed me her bag. I whispered "thanks" and he nodded.

It was obvious Henley had woken-up. But she pretended to still be asleep until we got to the truck. The fact that she was letting me carry her at all was a big relief.

"Ouch," she said when the cab light gave her a good look at my face.

I gave the automatic lie.

"It looks worse than it is."

I'd left Henley's drawing on the seat next to me. She picked it up and briefly looked at it before throwing it on top of the dash.

"Why do you like that so much?" she said.

"I don't know," I said. "I don't need a reason. I just do."

The two of us stared out the windows for a while. I didn't turn the ignition key. We needed a second to be ourselves again.

"Hey," I finally said. "In the back is stuff for root-beer floats. Up for a little midnight ice cream party?"

She smiled and nodded.

I started up the engine and pulled away from Gerald's. After a block or two I gave an exaggerated yawn.

"You know what?" I said. "I've been driving all day. Maybe you should take over."

Henley quickly slid over on the truck's bench seat, got up on her knees to see over the steering wheel and gripped it with both hands. She got a look of concentration on her face that always made me think of a monkey. I worked the pedals and had my knees at the ready to nudge the steering and generally keep us on the right path, but Henley was pretty good. We'd been doing this for years. There was a time she was small enough to sit in my lap, but that time had passed long ago. Soon she would be too old for this altogether. Maybe she already was. Maybe she was doing it just because she knew it made me happy.

And how could I not be happy? It was late at night and my daughter was guiding us home through weightlessly vacant streets. One of the many things you learned on the Bingerton Mine tour was that it was one of a handful of manmade things visible from space. I was never entirely sure why that was a good thing, but people seemed to think it was. One thing for sure, nobody was going to see Henley and me from outer space. But no matter, I'd put Henley's eyes up against any stars and in the bed of the truck we had melting ice cream that was as white as the moon.

MOTEL

(Camouflage John Updike, *Rabbit, Run*)

I.

They don't have a shot at competing with the wigwams and log cabins. Places for people who don't want their eight hours of sleep to be vacation time wasted. She's heard of one where there are ten-gallon hats for lampshades, you enter the bathroom through swinging saloon doors, and the gliding doors of the closet have painted bars like a jail cell, with a comical town drunk inside holding a jug marked XXX.

II.

Mr. Eccles, her boss, walks out on to the moist-hot pitch of the parking lot. He looks up at a sign with the word MOTEL stenciled across it. In the lower left corner, opposite POOL on the right, is COLOR TV--seven letters, each done in one of the seven different colors of the ROY G. BIV rainbow. He stands a long time rubbing the back of his neck while the sign wobbles against the flat blue of the desert sky. Mr. Eccles slaps his thigh. It's what he does when an idea strikes him. Two months later up goes Pete.

III.

Prairie Dog Pete is a glossy twenty-five-foot aluminum sign beckoning people into The Prairie Dog Motel. He's halfway out of his hole, an arm frozen mid-wave. His eyes sparkle like ice cubes. There is, however, something about Pete's facial expression that doesn't seem quite right. She thinks it's possible the look is meant to convey puzzlement. As if drivers will look at Pete and hear him thinking "You're so tired. The kids have been in the car for eight hours. Why on earth aren't you staying here?" Then they'll hit the brakes and make the turn. Maybe the sign just ran-up against the fixed limits of what the artist who made it was capable of. Mr. Eccles doesn't say anything and she doesn't ask. To her Pete looks carsick.

IV.

Dusk is now her favorite part of the day because she gets to turn on the switch with the piece of masking tape above it and the word "Pete." When the switch is flipped, Pete's previously dark silhouette suddenly bracelets the waxy night with lights the size of oranges.

V.

Business is good for a while. Then a new stretch of interstate side-steps their little ribbon of highway. Even though they are just twenty miles off, it may as well be a thousand. They get a respite when they're unofficially adopted by some of the local motorcyclists. People who prefer the scenic twists of the sinewy highway to the varicose interstate. The bikers stay up late revving their engines and listening to soft rock, like Phil Collins and Elton John. It scares families away. But the bikers are a steady source of income, that is until whatever it is in their blood that says "roam" speaks and they vanish. The bikers leave, but the families don't come back. They add options for weekly, then monthly rates. They attract only the occasional lonely soul, the motel honeycombed with empty rooms which she cleans everyday anyway.

VI.

A loud noise startles her at the desk one night. Two a.m.. Sounds something like a sneeze, although unless Pete has a cold, she can't imagine what could make a noise so loud. She goes outside and sees a hole's been cut in the chain-link around the swimming pool, which was drained two months ago for winter. She once read about a woman who killed herself with chopsticks. No joke. She took two chopsticks and rammed them through both ears. Even wore a kimono. This one looks like she used the diving board for extra altitude. Climbing up there with a toddler in one arm and a baby in the other must have been some feat. The three bodies lay face down on the chalky curve of the deep end.

Yelp! isn't going to let you bounce back from something like that.

VII.

Pete looks laughable, now. Not in a cartoonish way, but in a way that is scabby. He has a bad case of paint psoriasis, flakes of all sizes fall off him frequently and blow away into the desert. On the west side of the sign his face is convex, on the other, concave. Like he's been hit with a giant bowling ball. One eye is gone and deaf rust steadily gnaws away at his nostrils.

A crew of men come to tear Pete down with a crane shaped like a praying mantis. Its single pincer reaches out and grabs a chunk of Pete. The sign buckles like a beer can. Once a piece is wrestled off, the cab swivels and drops it in a dumpster. She's hoping when they're done they'll let her take home one of the lightbulbs; that is, if any survive the fall.

ALBUM

(Camouflage Don DeLillo, *Mao II*, Chapter 3)

Two decades of extremely rare and unannounced visits. The barest of human gestures. No apertures. Shutter-fast glimpses. No more real than the ghostly after-images a flash leaves in your eyes.

Travel was his great passion. Some of her earliest memories were of him at the kitchen table felt-tipping various routes on maps, or tacking charts to the living room walls. They moved—across states and then an ocean—five times before she was nine. But it wasn't enough. Like a surgeon with a bright knife, he had to use it. Wife, children, friends, eventually he severed them all.

When she was a teenager a small envelope with her name on it would sporadically arrive in the mailbox. No note, no return address, only photographs. Famous paintings, Roman walls, gardens, towers, coins, a funny cereal box, a house, a street during a downpour. In this way she pieced together where he was, or at least where he had been.

Photographs are mirrors confronting mirrors. He was always behind the camera. So while she was standing where he'd been standing—her eyes seeing through his eyes—when you turned the photo over there was just the word Kodak repeated over and over.

She put the 4x6s under the glistening, transparent sheets of a photo album. Placing them gently, delicately, like butterflies in a shadowbox.

She used the word "recluse" when people asked about him, even though the word she was reaching for was "eluder." It was difficult not to romanticize him. Remoteness is intrinsically beautiful.

Once she happened upon him in the room he used as an office. On the desk was a pile of unopened mail. Ignore the bills, they wouldn't be here long. On the ceiling were dozens of his balsa wood airplanes hung on invisible-thin lines. He was drinking coffee the color of the night sky. But tonight no wings or rudders. No uplifts or ballasts. Tonight he was sitting in the swivel chair holding a gun. When he saw her in the doorway, he loosened his face for his economical smile. He told her the gun was to ward off loss of faith and then put it back in a desk drawer.

Time doesn't show its face until the very end. A member of the hospital staff calls her sister with the news. As her sister relays details, she pictures a photograph of his dead body. His latest self-invention. Just another thing ending forever.

THEFT

(Camouflage J. M. Coetzee, *Foe*)

There are, after all, many holes. Doors, windows, even a chimney. So it is no surprise how easily the house is unopened for me. Once I'm inside the hardest thing is not to speak. The desire to speak is so strong that words feel like a secret behind my teeth. With silence I am not really there. I am a whimsical ghost. A smiling conjurer who paddles down the passages between rooms looking for something to steal. I have to steal. It is my raison d'etre. It's what gives authorship to what I do. Each thing I take is making marks of my presence on the soft paper of the rooms. I wish I didn't have to. Or that a thin coin from the higgledy-piggledy of scattered change on the dresser would be enough. But it needs to be noticed. Be read. When I steal I am created. I stand there as thin as the "l" between "word" and "worlds."

CANADIAN GIRLFRIEND

(Camouflage Tao Lin, *Eeeee Eee Eeee*)

Sara picks up an old pizza box and holds it out to the room like a newborn baby. "Wow," she says. "calling themselves just *Domino's*. They just caught up to that? Who in their life has ever said, 'Let's call Domino's Pizza? Do you get what I mean?"

We're in Shawn's apartment drinking, doing drugs, going blank a little. Everyone loves Shawn's place. It has great speakers, marshmallow sofas, a thick coffee table, and an amazing rug. Persian? Oriental? But the thing that makes the rug great is its size. It doesn't even technically fit into the room—the edges on two sides have to curl up and climb the walls for an inch or two.

"Is Justin here?" somebody says. "Does he know to come here? Somebody call Justin."

Among the people who are there is Bernadette. *Bernadette* seems like an impossibly long name. And rough for someone so smooth. She is literally what in these parts is usually proverbial. The girl from Canada. The one guys makeup when they claim to have a girlfriend but really don't. Like Canada is this impenetrable fortress that no one can ever penetrate to find out the truth. But her city is maybe seventy-five miles from ours and you could cross the border without a passport. She hasn't been here before. Someone brought her. Her boyfriend.

"OK, if no one else will, I'll call Justin."

"Fuck." This is spoken pretty loudly by Dwayne and not to someone, or even the room, but kind of to the universe. He is sitting, perfectly still, in a kitchen chair that he or somebody else has placed in the middle of the room. Dwayne outweighs each of us by at least a hundred and fifty pounds and looks like the kind of guy you'd expect to have the nickname "Moose." Maybe it's the buzzcut. Maybe it's because when he looks you in the eye you sense something bovine about it. He's cool and smart and so "Moose" would be a nickname that was not apt at all. But he needs a nickname. Screams out for one. Maybe I will give him one. I'm not sure what it might be, but it certainly won't be "Moose."

The girl from Canada, Bernadette, is sitting on the floor with her back against the wall. Just like I am but on the other side of the room. She's kind of beautiful. If people say eyes are the windows to the soul then hers are more like theaters.

"What is that when you feel like you're being filmed or are in a movie?" says Ellen. "Is it a feeling people had a hundred years ago or did film invent a whole new human emotion."

"Movies have been around for more than a hundred years," says Mark. "Like the 20's or something."

"1897," says Bernadette. It is the first word she has spoken.

"You know what I mean," says Ellen. "Do the Greeks have a word for it?"

"Embarrassment," someone yells at her from above somebody's head.

Bernadette picks up a big art book. I know it. I love it. I've passed out reading that book so often it feels like pajamas. I could go over there to the Canadian Bernadette and talk to her without telling her I'm paraphrasing the text next to the reproductions and the ideas would sound like they were my own.

A girl has been sitting cross-legged on the floor with a bunch of other cross-legged people and a bong. She starts laughing. Uncontrollable laughing. She gets up and goes into the kitchen. To spare the room and/or herself from the uncomfortable maniac quality of her laughter.

I think I remember hearing that the person who brought Bernadette from Canada is a singer and lead guitarist in a band. I look around the room for someone who looks like that. No one does. Or maybe it's that everybody does.

The girl in the kitchen is now laughing in a complex way.

It is the time of the party when words like Jesus and Schopenhauer are thrown around.

I look up at the ceiling. There is what I think is a motionless spider directly above me. After a while I realize it is a nail hole. If it was a spider it would be cool if Bernadette saw it too and the two of us would follow it across the ceiling and the spider would lead us to the bedroom.

"Is this The Beatles?" someone says.

No one answers.

"It sounds like The Beatles."

Shawn looks at the thermostat and turns it down.

There is a knock at the door and everybody's like "Oh shit."

"The cops," someone whispers.

"Why would the cops be here?" whispers someone else.

"My upstairs neighbors," hisses Shawn. "They don't like it when I play music too loud or for too long."

It shouldn't be a big deal. The drugs are easily pocketed and the thick cigarette smoke confuses the smell of pot. It's just that no one wants to *deal* with cops in the state they're in. Everybody looks around at everybody else.

A knock comes again, louder this time.

"Answer it," says Ann. "The longer we wait the more suspicious everything seems."

"Unless we wait them out."

I think about everybody quiet and motionless for hours. It would be kind of neat. Like performance art. At some point maybe I'd crawl across the room on my stomach like a soldier under barbed-wire and kiss Bernadette, the girl from Canada. Canada suddenly does seem far away. If not in miles then at least in the fact that it is a whole other country. Bernadette is a whole other country.

"Could it be Justin?"

"Did somebody call him?"

"Why doesn't he just walk the fuck in?"

But Shawn is emboldened by this new possibility and walks to the front door. When he opens it we've all been picturing cops for so long that for a split-second it seems like it really is a cop. But then the image dissolves into Justin.

"What the fuck?" he says. I assume because he was standing out in the hall for quite a while.

"We thought you were a policeman," Ann says.

"How fucked-up are you guys?" he says and heads for the bong table.

We are not fucked-up. We are drunk, depressed and grateful.

Bernadette has said nothing since the movie thing. She could be arrested at the U.S. border on her way home for being illegally shy.

"You are thrown into the something something of your life." Ellen is trying to remember lyrics. "Does anyone have any Pavement? There's a song about feeling like a movie."

The people in her immediate vicinity shake their heads no.

We are bored, crashed and sarcastic.

I've quit worrying that Canadian Bernadette is going to get creeped out by my watching her. I look at her now openly and steadily fantasize. *Buckle* is a strange word. Especially for such a basic thing. But then again if you say it aloud, like I just did in my head, it is almost onomatopoetic.

"An extra in the movie adaptation of the sequel to your life." Ellen has looked the lyrics up on her cellphone and holds it above her head triumphantly.

We are soft heads, pretentious, existentially optimistic.

A group gets up from the coffee table. They are leaving to

go to make and distribute pamphlets about something they've been talking about. I think I heard the words "moon hoax." The final pamphleteer walks out with the empty pizza box. He carries it out the door the way a waiter holds a tray. A pizza delivered in reverse.

The party is heading downward. It's only four people who are gone but it tilts things, like those wooden games with steel balls or marbles you sometimes saw or maybe got as a kid when you were on vacation with your family and stopped at an interstate gas station. Soon the music will be turned off and the television will be turned on. Then the only thing lower than TV, food, will quickly follow suit and become everybody's obsession. Cereal that comes with games on the back and a prize inside. Ramen noodles. Ice cream. Chinese food ordered in and teleported to the front door. Microwaving will take place. Or a trek to Denny's. Moons Over My Hammy.

I want to get up and take Bernadette my Canadian girl-friend a blanket that is draped on a chair next to me. I want to drape it across her. But gravity won't allow it.

We are strange, tender and silky. We echo.

"Terrorists," Moose yells.

I wish....

Then the feeling passes.

APOCALYPSE

(Camouflage Don DeLillo, *Mao II*, Chapters 12 & 13)

When the end came it was worse than science-fiction writers had ever imagined. Everywhere smelled bad because everywhere was a gravesite. Pigeons teemed. So did rats. They no longer felt the need to hide. Flashlight batteries were like a form of currency. Plastic bags served as makeshift caskets. Nobody had time to mourn. The feeling of being anonymous was abiding.

Rag-bodied people wore tattered t-shirts and frail sneakers. All the buildings fell down leaving the day-lit afternoons incandescent. What objects remained flashed like sparkly jewels. Cars were missing all their doors. Walls were spray-painted with ideas about sex. Memories. Human possibility.

The radiant sunsets were queer in their new-penny glow. There was milky green vomit. But no one was there to give it a name, to tell what it was a symptom of. The injured slouched. Heads gave away balls of hair. Each body was blurred by bruises. Mirrors were missing.

People used shopping carts as wheelchairs.

Many chose isolation. Others squatted in abandoned clusters.

Huddled nations where the strange ceremony of mumbled exchanges were still undertaken. News was often about history. Or muzzy rumors about the weather. There was a general lack of sense-making things. No one could formulate a design for the future that wasn't lethal.

INSOMNIA

(Camouflage Wallace Stevens, *Collected Poems*)

My body lies without shape in the silver moonlight which casts everything in the room blue. My mind follows the music of its monotonous babbling under stars and their alphabets of constellations. The clocks are black. Sleep hangs in front of me like a fat fruit. The empty night is perfection.

T.J. Gerlach is a Professor at Colorado Mesa University where he teaches creative writing and literature. He has an MFA from the University of Utah and a PhD from the University of Denver. His work has appeared in, among other places, *Juked, Flash Fiction Magazine, Aethlon, Shark Reef, Press, Literal Latte, The Wisconsin Review, Mid-American Review, Fiction Southeast, Think Journal* and *The Review of Contemporary Fiction.* He lives in Grand Junction, Colorado with his wife, the poet Jennifer Hancock.